NO **S** o**f**
MURDER

"A SHOCKER . . .
A GENUINELY ORIGINAL P.I. NOVEL."
Jeremiah Healy, Shamus Award-winning author of
THE STAKED GOAT

"POLISHED AND PROVOCATIVE . . .
A California mystery
of the hard-boiled school . . .
Thoroughly up to date and very well written,
with a corking good plot and fine characters."
Booklist

"CHILLING . . . SATISFYING . . .
Offers up tasty tidbits of San Francisco lore . . .
Russell is off to a good start."
The New York Times Book Review

"EXCELLENT . . . A WINNER . . .
NOT FOR THE SQUEAMISH"
Rendezvous

"REMARKABLE . . .
Russell's book hops from one to another milieu—
from avant garde theater to a deaf school,
from winos' alleys to an artist's studio,
to a double-twist conclusion."
The Armchair Detective

"A WISE BOOK, distilled from
a life's understanding of the human animal:
its limits, excesses, and, on occasion,
its surpassing beauty."
Loren D. Estelman, author of the
AMOS WALKER novels

NO SIGN OF MURDER

ALAN RUSSELL

AVON BOOKS ◆ NEW YORK

AVON BOOKS
A division of
The Hearst Corporation
1350 Avenue of the Americas
New York, New York 10019

First Avon Books Printing: June 1993

AVON TRADEMARK REG. U.S. PAT. OFF. AND IN OTHER COUNTRIES, MARCA REGISTRADA, HECHO EN U.S.A.

Printed in the U.S.A.

RA   10   9   8   7   6   5   4   3   2   1

To Laura

NO SIGN
OF
MURDER

1

"GOOD MORNING, SUNSHINE."

It wasn't my usual greeting, and it made Miss Tuntland laugh, a laugh that never failed to make me feel better.

"Good morning, Mr. Winter."

"Don't you think it's time you started calling me Stuart?"

"No."

"And why's that?"

"I've found that clients who have me call them by their first names are generally late on their payments. I think they feel first-name dispensation entitles them to a form of friendship, and being a friend means paying late—or not at all."

"Guilty as charged."

"So don't ask me to break rules just for you," she said, "even if all the other women in your life do."

"Miss Tuntland, you know you are the only woman in my life."

"I doubt that."

"Why?"

"Among other things, many other things, you had a call ten minutes ago from a Tammy Walters. Throaty voice, punctuated by meaningful breaths. The kind of voice that drives men wild."

"Like yours."

"The bill's still due on the first, Mr. Winter."

Miss Tuntland gave me the number, as she said, "with misgivings." She told me Tammy Walters had been referred by John Palmer, a fact I'd check before calling her back. Miss Tuntland had another call, so we said our good-byes. She was the most expensive answering service in the City, but would have been cheap at twice the price. She only had a dozen clients, clients assiduously screened before accepting their business. She took calls twenty-four hours a day, and did more juggling that a circus clown. I had never met her in person. Our lives crossed with the telephone wires. Like me, she didn't advertise. A friend of a friend had heard of this "marvelous disabled woman" who answered other people's telephones.

I never investigated Miss Tuntland, but she investigated me. When I called and inquired of her service, she not only didn't answer my questions, but had the gall to interview me. I found her technique interesting, and her questions odd enough to require honest answers. She told me that she had just dropped a client "for rudeness," and said she would consider my application. I remembered to say "thank you," and leapfrogged over a long waiting list. Why she accepted me as a client, and continued to put up with all the miscellaneous dirt that trailed me at the oddest hours, I didn't know, but I wasn't complaining.

Maybe she picked a private investigator for a client for vicarious thrills. Maybe she just liked my voice. I had learned long ago that some things are not worth investigating. Miss Tuntland's brain left most others in the starter's box, so I wasn't afraid of bouncing ideas off her. I didn't have a secretary, but she was so personable that everyone who called assumed she was one. She was my voice in the morning and at night, a conscience and a prod. She almost made me *like* the telephone.

I dialed John Palmer's work number. After getting through his secretaries, I identified myself. "This is Winter," I said.

"Yes," he answered, his words obviously constricted by the presence of others.

"I had a call from a Tammy Walters. She said you referred me."

"I did."

"When you are free to call, I would appreciate hearing about her."

"All right."

When John Palmer called back he was able to talk, even if he wasn't exactly gabby. "I've known Tammy and Terrence Walters for ten years," he said. "Terrence is one of Pillsborn, Monroe and Suture's expensive senior partners. You might have seen Tammy's picture on the *Chronicle's* social pages."

"I doubt it."

"She's a regular. She comes from an old San Francisco family with money, so she's always at the right party, and with the right face. Tammy has a perpetual smile like a three-way lamp: bright, brighter, brightest. So when she wasn't smiling at last Saturday's fund-raiser for the Rep Theatre, I knew something was wrong."

"Why wasn't she smiling? Bad manicure?"

"You really ought to get over your prejudice of the rich, Winter. It won't help your business."

"I know. Please continue."

"Her daughter's been missing for six months, since New Year's Eve. So I gave her your name."

"Did you tell her about your own difficulties?"

"No. Said a friend of mine swore by you."

Palmer wasn't inclined to talk more than necessary, so we said our good-byes. I don't tend to get too many Christmas cards from ex-clients, especially those who have needed their dirty underwear cleaned.

I dialed Tammy Walters. She had a Piedmont number, an Oakland suburb with big trees and bigger houses. A domestic answered the phone. "Mrs. Walters please," I said.

"Who is calling?"

"Stuart Winter."

Tammy Walters was the second person that morning who didn't want to advertise that she was talking to a P.I.

"Mr. Winter?"

"Yes."

"It isn't convenient for me to talk now, but I was planning on visiting the City later this afternoon. Would there be a good time for us to get together?"

We agreed upon the hour of three, and I gave her my office address on Geary. Miss Tuntland was right about the throaty voice. It hadn't driven me wild, but it was good enough to rank in the cheap-thrill category.

Tammy Walters proved to be an anticlimax to her voice, but then anything short of Garbo would have been. She was close to forty, and had a permanent tan. Her hair was artfully highlighted, which enhanced her light features. She had smile lines, but they didn't show while she was smiling or frowning, which she alternately did during most of our conversation.

"Mr. Winter."

She came forward without hesitation and extended her hand, a nice hand made more white and genteel in its coating of black sable. Her flesh was warm on a cold day, but sable coats have a habit of warming female parts. Twain hadn't said it, but he might as well have: 'The coldest winter I ever spent was a summer in San Francisco.' The statement and presence of her coat made my office smaller by half. I found Tammy a chair for her bottom and one for her coat. While I filed the paperwork, she surveyed the office and me. I noticed that her smile remained tentative. I agreed with her appraisal.

"May I get you a cup of coffee or tea, Mrs. Walters?"

She shook her fine coif with the slightest tilt and continued to look at me.

"Well, then, how may I help you, Mrs. Walters?"

"My daughter's been missing since New Year's, Mr. Winter. I'm told you have some expertise in these matters."

I chewed on the word for a second, and like an old dog at his bone decided to let out a small growl. "Experience is an ambiguous word, Mrs. Walters," I said, "but I'll use it in this example: it's been my experience that most people who are missing have made that choice on their own accord. And, if they have not broken any laws, and sometimes even if they have, I don't feel it is my business to go and find them."

"I don't know if any laws have been broken, Mr. Winter. I only know something must have happened to my daughter. Almost six months have passed now. I would have heard from her if she were all right."

"I don't have to ask if you've gone through the usual channels?"

"The police? They've been contacted. Too many times, they'll tell you."

"And what makes you think I can do more than they?"

"You come recommended. From two people. No one was willing to give details. They only said you gain results. I need a private investigator. That is what you are, isn't it?"

I nodded, but only after a moment's hesitation that didn't go unnoticed. "Did you wish to add something, Mr. Winter?"

I knew it would be easier to equivocate and be done with it, but chose the longer answer, anyway.

"Yes, I am a private investigator, Mrs. Walters. That's what my tax return says, and that's what I used to advertise in the *Yellow Pages*. But I don't like the implications of the title. If you buy me enough drinks I'll tell you that what I really am is a cleaner. I go into places and situations that are dirty and I try to clean things up. I don't take pix of husbands cheating on their wives. I don't track down witnesses to traffic accidents unless my creditors are calling. And I don't go looking for debutantes who have decided to walk away from their parents."

"Are you quite finished?"

"Quite."

"Then may I tell you about my daughter. Or do you have the need to make some more statements?"

I shrugged.

"Anita is nineteen years old," she said. She opened her mouth to say more, but had trouble beginning.

"A student?"

"She's taking a year off after high school. She's scheduled to attend Gallaudet College in Washington, D.C., this fall."

"Brothers or sisters?"

"None. She's an only child."

"Describe her personality."

"Independent. Spirited. That's why the police are sure she went off with somebody. But it's been six months . . ."

"Interests?"

"Everything, especially lately. Modeling. Wildlife. Politics."

"What kind of politics?"

"Human rights, especially the rights of the disabled. Anita is deaf."

There was an appropriate silence. I finally broke it.

"Do you have a picture?"

A snapshot slid across my desk. I picked it up. The promising voice of the mother was personified in the looks of the daughter. She had chestnut hair, green eyes that did a Sousa march, and cheekbones that perfectly bisected her brow. Her lips were indecently full and ran into dimples on both sides of her cheeks.

"You forgot to mention how beautiful she is," I said.

"I haven't mentioned many things about her."

"Let's hear them."

Tammy talked further. Anita had attended the Greenmont School for the Deaf, but by her mother's description she was special without the asterisk. I listened to her life, listened while I looked at her smiling face and dimples. Anita was last seen on December 31. It was her tradition to join the downtown throngs and bring in New Year's. Mrs. Walters said Anita had always enjoyed being a part of the midnight madness, was stimulated by all the vibrations in the air, and the activity. Anita was supposed to have met up with friends that night, but missed connections are common amidst all the North Beach New Year's chaos. Anita also no-showed for a party she had promised to attend, but that apparently wasn't unusual. Her reputation for independence was well established, enough so that it was a full week before anyone grew alarmed at her apparent disappearance. When Mrs. Walters's smile failed, and her mascara was three seconds from running, I spoke.

"I'll look into this, Mrs. Walters. If I take this case, you should know it's going to be expensive. It will cost you $3000 up front."

She nodded, her smile a little fuller now, able at last to categorize me as a mercenary, one of those expensive necessities of life. I didn't like that smugness. I didn't want her to think she was hiring a conscience, someone she could hold up to her friends and say, "I bought the best. I didn't spare expenses for poor Anita." So I cleared my throat for the sermon.

"You should know, Mrs. Walters, that cleaning is sometimes not a pretty process. When you cook, sometimes sauce spills on your oven rack. You can clean it up, but the job doesn't end there, it only begins, because suddenly you notice how dirty the rest of the rack is. So you take out the rack and scour it, and when that job is done, you put it back only to see how filthy the other rack is in comparison. Which forces you to clean the second rack, and I don't know if you've ever noticed, but two clean racks don't look like they belong in an oven that hasn't had a lot of elbow grease. So you clean the inside of the oven, make it spotless. And you think the job is finally over, but even while you are patting yourself on the back you notice fingerprints on the outside chrome of the oven, and no fingerprints ever seemed so obtrusive. The cleaning continues."

"Is there a point to this story?" she asked, the slightest edge of her cultured voice.

"Yes," I said. "Cleaning is dirty work. And even when you finish, things never shine exactly like you want."

2

"YOU PROMISED TO TELL me your theory, Stuart."

"I didn't promise you anything."

"You said you owed me for doing that evaluation. This is my day to collect."

"I said I'd buy you a drink. I didn't say I'd be one of your goddamn patients."

"I helped you on your case. And that wasn't the first time."

My one-word response was made acceptable to the tourists by the ringing of a cable car. Our dialogue had carried us east for ten blocks along Geary, from street people to the kind of people staying at the St. Francis who had streets named after them. Lefty O'Doul's was a welcome relief from both.

Norman excused himself for a visit to "the little boy's room," and when challenged, pretended not to be ashamed of his euphemism for the crapper. Phase one overcompensation, I supposed. Lefty's was quiet. The piano bar was on hold for later in the evening, and the work refugees hadn't yet arrived. I looked over the old baseball paraphernalia and allowed myself to sink a little bit into the vinyl. It was a good watering hole, not the best in the City, but a strong contender in my warped beauty contest. There was enough wood and history and spilled beers in its seams to make it pretty to me, enough pictures of stern men in baseball knickers to make me like it.

Norman arrived back at our table about the same time as our waitress. He tried to carry himself as tall and fit, but the inches he didn't have in his frame were in his stomach. As usual, he was stroking his well-trimmed beard. I had asked him on numerous occasions if that was psychologically significant, and he was fond of replying that sometimes a cigar is only a smoke. Norman probably owned a hundred different pairs of glasses, but all of them somehow managed to magnify and distort his dark eyes. He had attempted having contacts fitted about a dozen times, and each time had fled the optometrist's office in terror. It was a phobia, one of many, that he claimed to be actively working on. Perhaps because he didn't see well he looked harder than anyone else I knew.

I ordered my Scotch neat, and Norman did his oenological act and asked for some unpronounceable vintage. When the waitress had gone, Norman turned his glasses on me. "You asked for your Scotch neat," he said.

"I always ask for my Scotch neat."

"I know."

"Is that a crime?"

"No. An indicative pattern."

"And what pattern is that?"

"Everything is neat or clean to you. Compulsively so."

"You want to hear my theory?"

"You know I want to hear it."

"I think that virtually everyone who enters the field of mental health is missing a screw or two. They know they're not right in the head, and knowing they have their own quirks and illnesses makes them interested in others with the same."

Norman didn't look very impressed. "That's not an original theory, Stuart. And it's not the theory you promised to talk about."

Our drinks arrived, and I gratefully turned from Norman

to my glass. When I looked up I saw four eyes staring at me: Norman's two and his glasses. I sighed.

"A man wants an unadulterated drink, no rocks, no water. He asks for it neat. That is how it's done, Norman."

"You're evading," he said.

The Scotch made the telling a little easier. "I have observed in this world that there are three types of people. There are the cleaners, and there are those who make a mess, and then there are those who are weathervanes."

"Weathervanes?"

"Spinning in whatever direction the wind blows. Weathervanes constitute the bulk of our race. They wait for circumstance to change them. They never change circumstance. They never even think of changing it. They'll march for peace. They'll also be part of a lynch mob."

"It sounds like you have disdain for the average man."

"No. An understanding."

"And you—you're a cleaner?"

"It's just a way of thinking, Norman."

"You're being evasive again. I think for you it's more than a theory. It's almost a discipline—a religion, like cleanliness is next to godliness."

I sipped my Scotch and pretended interest in an old San Francisco Seals photograph. Norman wanted to play a different game of hardball.

"Am I wrong in thinking this is a way of life for you?"

"If you mean, do I get up every morning and say, 'Oh, boy, today I can go clean something,' then yes, you're wrong."

"You know that's not what I mean. If you think of yourself as a cleaner, you've given yourself a role. That being the case, you have chosen a way of life."

"Psycho-babble."

"Does being a cleaner make life easier?"

"No," I said, and the answer was too fervent, and too quick, and too telling. I would have bitten my lip but that would have given me away even more. Norman was a good shrink, but not good enough to hide the smile on his face. He had his answer.

"I'm paying for the drinks, Norman," I said. "Not for analysis."

We stopped talking for a minute, which meant I drank my Scotch too quickly and ordered another. But we had been friends and sparring partners too long to stay quiet.

"How'd that case go this morning?" asked Norman. "Did you get your man?"

I nodded, but spared him the details. Mrs. August Sinclair had hired me to do an assets check on her husband Gus. She wanted a divorce, and she wanted money. Gus had claimed a desire for the former, and a lack of the latter. My investigation had proved that Mrs. Sinclair would ultimately be a very rich divorcee, but Gus disappeared before my client was granted all her wishes, vanished even before being served with divorce papers. Gus apparently wanted to delay the inevitable as long as he could. Maybe he thought that given a little extra time he could better hide his assets. More likely, he wanted to drive his wife batty. Marital bliss turned to martial arts.

It had taken me the better part of a week to find Gus. When we finally met face to face, he thought I was a potential investor in one of his enterprises. A smart server doesn't wait. A smart server doesn't gloat, I knew that, but I also knew I shouldn't drink, or eat red meat, or hang around with women who regularly use their middle name. I smirked while I served him with the papers, and then he tried to serve me with his fist—it had almost served me right.

"What about Dr. Cohen's caseload?" I asked. "Working on any cover material for *Psychology Today?*"

"Not exactly," said Norman, "But there is this new patient who comes in with his dog. He talks more to him than he does to me. He says he understands all animals, and is fluent in their tongues. I've heard him talk to his dog. Barks and growls and snarls."

"Is he functional?"

"He's a urologist."

I thought I hid my smile behind my glass but Norman saw it.

"What's so funny?"

"I was just wondering how he'd approach me for my specimen. I can just hear him say, 'Could you please go into that little room and lift your leg?' "

Norman stifled a laugh. "I shouldn't tell you about my patients," he said, "It's not only the ethics, it's how you make me look at things. I can just see how you'd handle this case. You wouldn't ask him how he felt, you'd go and feel his nose."

"Only if his bark was worse than his bite."

Norman raised his hands. "Don't say anything else, Stuart. It's not fair."

"And I would think it only prudent to spread newspapers all over your office carpeting."

Norman was pinching himself, but it wasn't working. His sides were starting to shake.

"I wouldn't tempt his olfactory senses, either. Better keep your backside turned."

"I'm probably going to have to refer him to someone else now," said Norman. "You have a habit of leaving images in my mind."

I refrained from saying that was a doggone shame. We talked about little things for a few minutes. Dr. Norman Cohen was a friend of almost ten years, one of the few who had survived my rise and fall. We looked at our watches at about the same time.

"Back to the dog-eat-dog world," I said.

We walked to the door and said our good-byes outside. There was a cab dropping off a couple at the Hotel Stewart, and Norman went to commandeer it. He had his office in a high-rise building on Van Ness, clustered with other well-heeled professionals. You didn't necessarily have to be crazy to see Norman, just rich.

I walked over to Union Square and sat down on one of the usually crowded park benches. The cold spell had scared off the fair weather crowd. The Square was quiet save for the rock doves, better known as pigeons, or flying rats. As a card-carrying Audubon sort, usually anything in feathers grabs my attention, but my devotions are drawn at pigeons. A dozen of the feathered panhandlers approached me, and then a dozen more, but they gave up when I didn't make any offerings. They hadn't looked very hopeful anyway, had acted out the charade like old hookers who know their propositions aren't going to be accepted. You can't teach an old hooker new tricks. Or get her to turn them either. Nearby, two bums shared a bottle of Thunderbird. Pigeons haven't yet developed that kind of thirst. Give them time.

Pro-Union demonstrations had been held in Union Square before the Civil War, and had earned the park its name. The years hadn't quieted the speech-makers or the causes, and Union Square never lacked either. But it didn't look like the revolution was going to start on this Monday; it was called off on account of the weather.

A woman joined me on my bench and I surveyed her in a glance: Forty, well off, probably resting before taking a little cable car, as Tony Bennett crooned, "halfway to the stars." Her bags bespoke the offerings of Nordy's and Needless-Markups, a red flag for more than pigeons. Two spare-change hustlers approached her and started their pitch.

"Beat it," I said before she reached for her purse.

They looked at me, and made two decisions, one wrong and the other right: that I was with her, even if I wasn't sitting next to her, and that they should heed my advice and beat it.

The woman was also making her appraisal of me. Her eyes appeared nicely made up even when they glowered. The wind blew her scent at me, and I sniffed appreciatively.

"Why did you do that?"

"I've seen those two before. The one with the greasy hair and stubble is trouble. He likes to roll winos. Maybe spare change would have been enough today. Maybe you could have bought their good will with a dollar. But your full purse would have tempted them, and they might have snatched it."

She looked at me, suspiciously pulled her purse to her chest, then stood up to leave. "Thank you," she said uncertainly.

3

I RENTED AN OLDS with unlimited mileage, a full-size model with a big engine. My pickup needed some engine work, enough to put me in the rental market. Everyone says it doesn't make sense to have a car in San Francisco, and just about everyone still puts his car in long-term parking that's about as expensive as monthly payments on a Cadillac. My rental had plenty of interior room, more than I was used to. I stretched out and enjoyed the ride, despite the traffic tie-up on the way to the Bay Bridge.

I like Oakland even if no one else in San Francisco does. Gertrude Stein's putdown of Oakland is forever on the lips of San Franciscans: "There is no there there." But Oakland does have some parking spaces. I found one directly in front of Ellen Reardon's house.

Hers was a nice cottage surrounded by too many apartment buildings, but with a crack of a view out to Lake Merritt. A little garden lined the path, with a few annuals, a few perennials, and two jacaranda trees that showed their lavender hairdos proudly. I could hear the geese honk in the direction of the lake as I pressed the doorbell. There was no sound except the geese, so I pressed again and once more heard silence. I had raised my fist and started a tattoo when the door opened, and I'm not sure which looked more stupid, my hanging hand or my expression.

Inside the cottage a lamp blinked on and off. A pixieish young woman with a smile bigger than her frame stood at

16

the door. She had long hair, an upturned nose, and a nonoffensive cheerleader demeanor. She was cute when she glowed, and she'd be comely when she was serious.

"Impatient, are we?" she said.

"No, just stupid," I answered, and she laughed at that, and laughed a little more when I used my hanging hand to knock at my head. Only I could hear the hollow. Ellen Reardon was deaf.

"Mr. Winter?"

"Yes."

"Please come in."

I slowly followed her inside, stopping to admire the needlework that lined the walls. There were colorful embroidery and needlepoint projects. In the living room a quilt was in its final stages, all bright colors and blending patterns. I knew that quilts like this rarely warmed bodies. They were hung in fancy homes and called art. I touched it, glad to find that Ellen had put enough batting in it to still make it functional.

"Very nicely done," I said.

"Mr. Winter, I'll need you to face me in order to understand what you're saying."

I'm not much for blushing, but I think I came close. "Sorry," I said. The word came out much too loudly. I modulated my speech but was sure I overmouthed my words enough to make me look like someone suffering denture fallout. "I was saying I liked it."

"Thank you." Ellen raised her long and full hair and briefly exposed her ears and two small hearing aids. It was supposed to be informative, but I couldn't help finding it sexy. "I am not severely deaf," she said, "but I can't pick up very much. Mostly I lip read. I am very good at that. I can understand about sixty percent of your words that way."

"Which is probably sixty percent more than you'd want," I said. If she understood the joke, she didn't laugh.

"Mrs. Walters said you were investigating Anita's disappearance," said Ellen, doing my job.

"Yes. Mrs. Walters said you probably know Anita better than anyone. I need your knowledge."

"What, in particular?"

"Everything and anything. She told me you lived with Anita for three years at the Greenmont School. You observed her. You heard her secrets. Best friends know things."

"Yes," said Ellen, "best friends do."

There was a lot of coolness in her statement.

"Weren't you two best friends?"

"At one time."

"And what happened to change that?"

"We fought."

"Over what?"

"Things. We had a big fight just before she graduated. I haven't talked to her since."

"What did you fight about?"

Ellen sighed. It wasn't a memory she liked. But she talked to me and my notepad anyway.

"We fought over my boyfriend, or what was once my boyfriend. Anita decided we should share him without asking me. It wasn't something I was happy to find out about."

I made tsk, tsk sounds, and then realized a lip reader wouldn't pick them up. "Bad surprise."

"Bad, yes, but not really a surprise."

"No?"

"You know what Anita looks like."

"Only by picture," I said. "You're supposed to tell me more than a glossy."

Ellen didn't look thrilled by the prospect. "Am I supposed to do that with, or without, my talons?"

I made a retracting motion.

"Anita likes to be the center of attention," she said.

"She's not happy unless she's turning heads. Usually she doesn't have to work at it."

"Did she have boyfriends?"

"Our room was like a florist's shop."

"Any steady?"

"No. She's always kept her distance. She likes going out, but I don't think she likes intimacy. I tried to talk to her about sex a few times, but she changed the subject."

I liked talking with Ellen. She didn't mince words, and she was an attentive listener. I also found myself beguiled by her speech. It was almost as if she talked with a foreign accent. Some of her words weren't distinct, and some were mispronounced or accented the wrong way. It was as if English wasn't her native tongue, and in reality it wasn't. That she could respond almost immediately to my questions made her accomplishment all the more amazing. She told me, with not a little pride, that she had graduated at the top of her class at Greenmont, and that she had been determined to join the mainstream of the hearing world. But like someone going from one culture to another, she retained telltale habits. Her native tongue was sign language, something she unconsciously adopted many times in her speech. Her hands were expressive, a digital ballet for my eyes.

"Do you know whether she continued seeing your boyfriend?"

"I don't know. I doubt it."

"Why?"

"She's never stayed long with any boy. Or man."

"Mrs. Walters described Anita as being spirited."

"She is."

"Could she just have taken off somewhere?"

Ellen thought about the question for a minute. "Maybe," she said. "I really don't know."

"Tell me something else about her."

"She's a perfectionist, and she's stubborn."

"How so?"

"She won't talk. She refuses to."

"Why?"

"Deaf people know our speech doesn't sound normal. Everything about our talking is an acquired skill. There's a lot to our learning how to speak, and there's a lot of frustration. Anita told me she hated all the lessons. I think she eventually rebelled against them in her own way."

"What kind of lessons? And what was her own way?"

"You'd have to be deaf to understand," said Ellen, dismissing my question.

"That's like being told you have to be a certain color to understand racial problems."

"And maybe that's true. Have you ever participated in a disabled awareness session?"

"No."

"You ought to. The school offers them to parents of deaf children. They get an earful, or lack of it."

"How about giving me a primer?"

"How about giving up your ears? It's a different world, and you'd have to be born again without any knowledge of sounds to really hear what I'm saying. Tell me what you know about deaf people."

"They don't hear," I said. "And they read lips."

Ellen shook her head. "A lot of deaf people don't read lips," she said. "Because they don't hear what sound lips make, many can't read lips as well as the hearing. We have to deal with stereotypes like that all the time."

"Forgive my ignorance then," I said. "Give me some lessons on being deaf."

Against her better judgment Ellen smiled. "You accept our talking as something natural," she said, "but I see it as an accomplishment. I'm lucky—I can hear some sounds— but the lessons were still hard for me. At Greenmont they believe in teaching students total communication. That means they try to develop language competence in all ways. Imagine being able to see words but not hear them. I sat through countless hours of fish exercises, instructors opening and closing their mouths, and me doing the same."

She reached for my throat and rested her hand on my larynx. I swallowed involuntarily. "Talk to me," she said.

"Your hand feels nice," I said. "Your fingers are strong, much stronger than most women's. Must be your work."

Ellen removed her hand. Slowly. "I could feel your words," she said, "by feeling your throat. That was just one of many exercises in school. That was a way of teaching us how to talk. Throat vibrations. I like the feel of your voice, Mr. Winter."

I didn't reach for her larynx, but I was sure I'd like her throat, too. I think she read my face, which caused me to reach for my throat and clear it. We both laughed. "Tell me," I emphasized, "about some other exercises."

"There's 'mirror, mirror, on the wall,' " she said.

"Which is?"

"Facing the mirror all day and repeating words."

"Not much fun."

"It was Anita's favorite. She liked her reflection very much. She complained about most of the other lessons, thought they were degrading. It shows in her speech. She learned to be a good lip reader, but not a very good speaker. So she didn't talk."

"Deaf and dumb, then."

"Not an acceptable term. Neither is mute. Virtually all deaf people have voices. She chose to be nonverbal. That's not an uncommon choice."

"Why?"

"Where do you think the expression 'dummy' comes from? The implication still stands today. If we don't sound right, we're slow, aren't we? And since we have a hard time modulating, that makes us that much more suspect. Do you know how many blowing exercises I had to endure in learning how to differentiate between a shout and a whisper?"

She obviously had learned her lessons. Ellen's voice was close to a shout. I moved the subject back to Anita. "So she chose to be nonverbal?"

"Yes. Deaf people have a lot of pride. Some deaf people have a chip on their shoulder. Anita has both. Some of the deaf choose to be expressive with their gestures rather than fail in speech. They prefer to not speak, so as to not give the hearing an opportunity to make judgments. American Sign Language, Ameslan, is a wonderful and descriptive language. Among the deaf, Anita is very articulate. But when she was with the hearing she wouldn't speak. She didn't want to give them the opportunity to call her stupid. Anita preferred they think her snobby or haughty, a being who didn't deign to talk."

"You haven't forgiven her, have you?"

"No. She has so much. She didn't need to toy with Darren."

"Your boyfriend?"

"Ex."

"What's his last name?"

"Fielder."

"Mrs. Walters said Anita had a number of interests. Tell me about them."

"Did you know she was a model?"

"Not the particulars."

"It was a good profession for her. It allowed her to look at her portfolio almost as much as she did her mirror."

"Was that a tough choice?"

"For her, yes."

"Did she work for an agency?"

"Sort of. An agency of one, I think. His name was Kevin Bateson. He was always taking her out on sessions."

"Was he a boyfriend?"

"One of many."

"Was he successful in placing her?"

"A bit. Everyone at Greenmont got a little sick of her displaying this one cold-cream ad."

"What about hobbies?"

"When she was a senior she decided to be a rebel with a cause. She volunteered for gorilla training."

"Guerrilla training? As in rebels?"

"Gorilla." Ellen made the sign in sign language, then pantomimed, walking on knuckles, blowing out her cheeks, and beating her chest. "See how miscommunication wouldn't occur as often if everyone signed?"

I was still laughing at her gorilla imitation. She continued talking, this time without beating her chest.

"Up in the Berkeley Hills they've been teaching some gorillas sign language. Anita was actually dedicated to that project. She went once or twice a week."

I had heard about the work. It was controversial. It upset some people to think that animals could use language to communicate. There were reports that the gorillas talked back, even lied on occasion, and we've always wanted the corner on the deception market. We don't like our cultural toes stepped upon, especially by feet that are substantially larger than our own. I made another note on a pad that was growing heavy with them.

"Mrs. Walters also said Anita was political."

"That happened during her senior year. Remember that chip on her shoulder? It grew worse. Anita was convinced that people with disabilities didn't get a fair shake. She thought we were abused. She used that sign a lot. So she circulated some petitions and said she was going to change things."

"Change what?"

"Attitudes I guess. Which are about as easy to change as the tide."

I hid my smile. Joe Friday in search of just the facts. "How did she get along with her family?"

"Just so-so, I'd say. She didn't go home very much. In her junior and senior years I don't remember her going home at all to see her parents. She was angry about something, but never said what."

"No hints?"

"Not really."

"How did they treat her?"

"In checkbook terms, they spoiled her rotten."

"Were her parents affectionate to her?"

"No. They were always reserved."

I clicked my pen and put it away. "You've been very patient, Ellen," I said. "There's a lot to Anita."

Ellen surveyed me with her calm eyes. "There's a lot to me, also."

"I know that," I said. "I'll probably have to bother you again."

"It was no bother."

I think I knew that, too.

"Do you like being a private detective?"

"Sometimes."

"It must be exciting."

I stood to leave. "Thank you very much," I said. "How do you say 'thank you' and 'good-bye' in sign language?"

Ellen showed me the signs. "Good-bye" was easy, a simple wave. "Thank you" wasn't much harder. It was similar to blowing a kiss. I signed my thanks. I'm not sure if I blew Ellen a kiss, and I'm not sure whether she signed "thank you" back, or blew me a kiss. I suspected sign language had as many ambiguities as speech, and wondered if I was punning already with my digits. Or flirting. Likely both.

I paused at the quilt before leaving. This time I remembered to face Ellen. "It really is beautiful," I said. "How much will you be selling it for?"

"Eight hundred dollars," she said.

I whistled.

"But everything's negotiable."

I wondered, briefly, how someone who couldn't really hear could put such intonation and meaning in her words.

4

I LOOKED FORWARD TO taking the Olds on the open road, but the open road no longer exists anywhere near San Francisco. I drove on 101 south down the peninsula. Once there were communities separated by little boundaries, but now everything was merged. Burlingame, San Mateo, Redwood City, Palo Alto, Mountain View, Sunnyvale—all looked the same from the freeway.

Greenmont didn't look any more enticing from 101, but after making my escape from the road I found some verdant growth and a few open spaces. The school appealed to my senses even more. It was clean, well landscaped, and, yes, quiet. I went to the administrative offices and asked the receptionist if the school counselor could spare a few minutes with me. I was asked about my business, and appraised by orbs that made a raptor's look charitable. I volunteered as little information as possible, and tried to make long with Dale Carnegie smiles and patter. The glib words literally fell on deaf ears, the loss of which the receptionist made clear was a blessing in my case. Grudgingly she finally moved herself from her chair and approached a woman standing nearby. After my request was signed, I was judged by two sets of frowns, and then a further conversation in hand talk. When you are the topic in a language you don't understand, paranoia generally sets in rather quickly. Their talk lasted another minute, which is twenty minutes in paranoia time, before the second woman approached me.

"I'm Mrs. Lockhart," she said, her voice quite intelligible but with the intonational giveaways of the deaf.

"I'may Uartstay Interway."

It wasn't the smartest introduction. It was in fact a petty statement, but Pig Latin is my only other tongue. It was one that Mrs. Lockhart didn't know, or pretended not to acknowledge. An iceberg about the size of the one that sunk the *Titanic* stared me down.

"I'm Stuart Winter," I said. "I'm here on behalf of a client. There's a matter I'd like to discuss in private."

Mrs. Lockhart motioned for me to follow. She was in her forties, but appeared well built even in a business suit. Her face was unadorned, and her manner serious. We went into her office, and by the sign on her door I saw that she was vice principal. Her office was on the stark side, and matched her manner.

"What may I help you with, Mr. Winter?"

"I'm a private investigator, Mrs. Lockhart. I've been hired by the Walters family to find their daughter Anita. I'm sure you know that she's missing."

"Yes."

"Would you have any idea where she is?"

"No. And I'm not at all sure this is a subject I should be talking to you about."

"Why's that?"

"You claim to be something. I've seen no proof."

I passed her my card. When she took her eyes off it, I continued talking. "Please feel free to call Mrs. Walters," I said. "She'll corroborate my story."

Mrs. Lockhart pushed my card back, not wanting it or me in her office. "Schools are sanctuaries, Mr. Winter. I'm not very inclined to answer your questions even with the consent of Mr. and Mrs. Walters."

I ignored that. "Mrs. Walters believes that Anita's in trouble."

"I have always found Anita very capable of handling herself."

"You don't think she's in trouble then?"

"I think she's probably in Rio doing a photo session."

"Why Rio?"

"Why not? I understand it's hot there. Hot water is her natural element."

"And who's doing the shooting? Kevin Bateson?"

"More than likely." Her lips curled in disgust.

I made my first guess. "I heard you had trouble with him."

"Who told you that?"

Second-guessed means second guess. "I heard you talked with him, threatened him even."

"It wasn't so dramatic as that. I just told him that he was interfering with Anita's studies. She did poorly her junior year because of him."

"What about her senior?"

"She didn't associate much with him. She had other interests." The last word was emphasized a little too fully.

"Too busy spending time with Darren Fielder, I guess."

Mrs. Lockhart credited me with an almost imperceptible highbrow sneer. "You have been busy, haven't you, Mr. Winter? But Darren was much more preoccupied with Anita than she was with him. I suppose you know that already, though?"

"I'm visiting Darren after this. I'll let him tell me."

"Give him my regards," she said. "Tell him we're all proud of his progress."

Job or school? "It's a nice job to have landed so young," I said.

Mrs. Lockhart gave a maternal nod. "Computers are for the young. We have a strong program."

"I've heard. He's doing well by Data-Link."

"Has he left Cube Tech already?"

"No," I said quickly. "My mistake. But back to Anita. Was she a trouble to you?"

"Anita had her own mind," she said. "She changed rather dramatically. As a sophomore she was very reserved. Some time during her junior year she realized how pretty she was. And as a senior she was something of a rebel."

"What was she rebelling against?"

"Authority, I suppose."

"Any guesses why?"

"No."

"She worked with gorillas."

"Yes." Mrs. Lockhart almost smiled. I wondered if she liked hair, and whether I should open my shirt. "She got credit for that, and she enjoyed it very much."

"What else did she enjoy?"

"Her privacy," she said pointedly. "And I really don't think I should violate it any further."

She rose. I continued to sit. "I'd like to see her records. Short of that, I'd like to discuss them."

"Out of the question."

"I know the Privacy Act," I said. "It doesn't prohibit our conversing about her background."

"It does if I say so."

"Are there things about Anita you don't want me to know? Are there things that would embarrass this school?"

"I have to go to a meeting, Mr. Winter."

I finally got up. "Why was Anita nonverbal?"

"Because people like you are so judgmental. Do I criticize you because you can't sign? Or even if you did, would I think less of you because you'd do it haltingly? The hearing are not very understanding."

I decided not to get defensive. "It's my job to ask questions."

"And I have a job of my own to attend to."

I followed her out the door. We said our good-byes, and I walked away. My ears burned, and I turned to see who was talking about me. Two sets of hands were working furiously, Mrs. Lockhart's and the receptionist's. I had the distinct feeling I wouldn't be welcomed back.

Sunnyvale is the heart of Silicon Valley. Once upon a time, before nanoseconds and megahertz, in the days of I LIKE IKE and *I Love Lucy,* Sunnyvale was mostly an agricultural community. Orchards abounded, and some of the most fecund land in the world produced a multitude of crops in that sunny valley. But asphalt and concrete became the order of the day when the silicon chip began its reign. Sunnyvale grows computers now, not apricots and cherries.

Finding Cube Tech was no easy task. I knew the building, or thought I did, but others had grown up like it, and everything looked the same. High tech might have spawned computer drafting, might have been the biggest boon to architecture since the arch, but Frank Lloyd Wright didn't have any competition in Sunnyvale's buildings. Cube Tech was old by Valley terms, almost two decades, so I guessed it would be in the center of the sprawl, but it was soon clear I didn't know where I was going. I stopped at a phone booth to get the address and make a few calls.

Miss Tuntland didn't sound pleased to hear my voice. She gets that way when I don't check in regularly.

"What grand occasion prompts this call?" she asked.

"National Answering Service Day."

"I am sure that was yesterday," she said pointedly.

"I've been working."

"On whom?"

Her voice was more than suspicious. I liked an indignant Miss Tuntland.

"Tammy Walter's daughter," I said. "She's been missing for six months."

Not totally convinced. "Uh huh."

"Which means that we have a lot of work cut out for us."

"We?"

She didn't squawk too indignantly, so I kept talking.

"First, call Mrs. Walters," I said. "Tell her I've accepted the case and that I'll need payment by the end of the week. Also, tell her that I want to meet with her husband as soon as possible. She said he works in the City. I'll go to his office or he can come to mine."

"You've fumigated?" she asked.

"And the other meeting I need you to set up . . ."

The overdue protestation finally occurred. "Hey!" she said. "Remember me—the one who's just supposed to answer your phones?"

"Flowers," I said, "roses even, a San Francisco tradition. Belated offerings for National Answering Service Day."

There was a long moment of silence. I upped the ante. "And chocolates, too. All sent tomorrow."

"Long-stem," she said, "and Ghirardelli chocolate. No substitutions."

"No substitutions."

"Okay, what else?" Her voice was definitely mollified. I would even have guessed pleased.

Normally an investigator doesn't allow anyone else to set up an appointment. Sometimes one call is all you'll get; sometimes the proper phone technique saves you a trip. But I trusted Miss Tuntland to make my professional calls, which was another way of saying I trusted her with my life.

"I'll need you to call the Gorilla Project and set up an appointment with its director."

"The Gorilla Project?"

"As in apes."

"Located where?"

"Up in the Berkeley Hills."

"And who should I ask for, Fay Wray?"

"Enough monkey business, Miss Tuntland. Tell them I need to visit at a time convenient for them. Tell them I'm investigating the disappearance of Anita Walters."

"Okay."

"Any calls?"

"Several. I discouraged one or two. But B&H called. They've something for you. Your contact is Denise."

"I'll call later." B&H was Bradford & Hall, attorneys at law. The firm was a big one. They paid for most of my necessities, and a few of my vices.

"Mr. Winter?"

Miss Tuntland had her quiet voice on.

"Yes?"

"Is this a dangerous case?"

"No. Piece of cake."

"Good," she said, "because I still haven't gotten your check."

It was our way to mask concern. I made some mild remonstration, and she faked umbrage, and we hung up on one another. I dropped more change into the phone and dialed another number by memory.

"San Francisco Public Library."

"Special Collections, please."

The connection went through.

"Special Collections. This is Leland Summers."

"This is Winter."

"And just when I was wondering whether you were still alive. I wondered whether Winter disappeared in the summers. I've wondered about that a lot."

He was using his teasing voice, full-throated, almost echoing on every word, and indignantly exclamatory.

"Keep dreaming," I said.

He laughed. Lee was a homosexual. I was still reluctant to use the word gay even after all these years. I hated the discontinuance of a good Anglo-Saxon word because of the association with it. I accepted homosexuals, if not with open arms, then at least a relatively open mind. In San Francisco if you wanted to love thy neighbor, that was a necessity.

"Well, winter, spring, summer, or fall," he prattled, "I'm just glad you took the time to call." Leland liked the extremes in our names. He also liked the extremes in our persons.

"I need a favor, Lee. I was wondering whether you could gather together some material on the deaf."

"Do I hear correctly?"

I sighed. "Yes."

"Anything in particular?"

"Just your usual eclectic best."

"When do you need it?"

"Today might be six months too late. I'll buy you a drink for your efforts. Maybe even some dim sum."

"Drinks, yes. I'll have to check with Joe about the other."

I had to laugh. "He's not still jealous?"

"Yes. Maybe I should have spared him my fantasies."

I was liberal, but not that liberal. "Maybe you should spare me, too," I said. "In fact, you'd better."

Lee laughed, happy he had nettled me. "I'll be free at five."

"B of A?"

"Good."

I was lucky to find Cube Tech's address in a cannibalized phone book, and made my usual curses to a world indifferent to the needs of others. The plant wasn't far away, and even had an open space in its visitor parking. A security officer stopped my entry to the building. He was a big, beefy fellow, probably a tool-user, but I wouldn't take bets.

"I'm here to see Darren Fielder," I said.

"Are you expected?"

"No."

"What's your name?"

"Stuart Winter."

The man consulted his sheet, and looked for my name. I wondered if he was really reading or faking it.

"Maybe you could give Mr. Fielder a call," I said, "and tell him that a friend of a friend is here to see him."

There was a long beat, as if the man was on a time delay, and then he answered. "Okay."

I was escorted to a waiting area. A variety of tech magazines littered the table and I picked one up. Darren Fielder rescued me from my ignorance somewhere in the third paragraph of the lead article. He was a young man who already had the severity of one who is old. He had short hair, large glasses, and the unsmiling manner of someone disturbed in the midst of something important.

I made my introductions and handed him my card. "What do you want?" Direct.

"Anita Walters."

"You've come to the wrong man."

"Which would be the right one?"

"Maybe Mr. Harrady. Will Harrady. Maybe someone else. Not me."

"Who's Will Harrady?"

"He was an English teacher at Greenmont."

"And what happened to him?"

"Maybe you should ask Anita."

"Maybe we should stop playing games."

Our conversation slowed. He took time to think and I didn't like that. "Why are you talking to me?"

"You weren't first. I talked with Ellen Reardon. And Mrs. Lockhart. One of them wished you regards."

His face contorted with anger. "You're a funny man, aren't you, Mr. Winter? Well, welcome to the triangle. Or should I say quadrangle? Or do you plan to join? Will it be a quintuple?"

"I suppose that depends on whether Anita Walters is still alive."

My remark shook him a little, enough for him to turn his head from my unpleasant lips. Like Ellen, he had two hearing aids, so I assumed he could pick up some of my words, but I left him in silence while he collected his thoughts. "I'm sure she's alive," he finally said, more to himself than anyone.

I stepped into his line of vision. "Who's Will Harrady?"

"He was an English teacher at Greenmont."

"You already said that. What happened to him?"

"There were only rumors . . ."

"Tell me about them."

"They're second hand. I graduated two and a half years ago. It happened eight or nine months ago."

"Shoot."

"I heard he suddenly left the school. Officially he resigned, but no one believes that."

"What do they believe?"

"I heard Anita always stayed after class. She supposedly always . . . always played up to Mr. Harrady. They say Mrs. Lockhart caught them kissing. They also say Mrs. Lockhart was involved with Mr. Harrady."

"They were caught in the same way Ellen caught you and Anita?"

He blushed. "Sort of. We were together, and we looked guilty. At least, I looked guilty."

"How did Ellen respond?"

"She was very upset. We're the same age and we'd been together for a few years. We'd even talked about marriage."

"The two of you were discovered after the Mr. Harrady incident?"

He nodded.

"And Ellen wasn't forgiving?"

"Maybe she would have been if I hadn't been so taken by Anita. But I was."

"What happened between you and Anita?"

"Anita never cared for me like I did for her. I was the one who pursued her. She's so pretty. I don't even know why she went out with me. Maybe because I was older and away from the school. Maybe because I was persistent."

"Were you ever intimate with her?"

Darren reddened again. "That's none of your business."

"It is."

He had to think. He was a whiz in some fields, but a novice in others. "Once. Sort of."

"Tell me about the once. And the sort of."

"It happened just before Anita left Greenmont. I took her to a fancy dinner one night, white tablecloths and all. I'd planned our special night together for a month. I'd even sent her flowers the entire week before our date. After dinner we went to a foreign film with subtitles. Then we drove around San Francisco. At around midnight we parked at Coit Tower. We looked at the view for a while, and then I tried kissing her, but she wouldn't. She just turned away. That got me mad, and I told her so. Then she told me to go ahead and kiss her. So I did, but it was like kissing my hand."

"And did that make you mad, also?"

"Just more frustrated. It wasn't like she was doing anything wrong. It was just that she wasn't reacting."

"So what did you do then?"

"I started taking her clothes off. But she still didn't react. It was like she wasn't there. She was so beautiful, but so cold."

"Did you have sex with her?"

"I tried . . . but I couldn't. She was just so . . . cold."

"Did you continue seeing her?"

"Not very much. After she graduated she started hanging around with a new crowd."

"What kind of crowd?"

"Artists, she said; phonies, I say."

"Where did you see her?"

"In her apartment. Her parents set her up in a place on Russian Hill."

"And you saw her new friends?"

"Both times I visited, other people were there. I never stayed long."

"Did she talk—sign—about anyone in particular?"

"No."

"Did you notice anyone that stood out?"

"No."

"Why this new crowd? Was she interested in art?"

"I don't think so. She modeled for some of them."

I made a few entries on a pad, then put my pen down and raised my eyes to his. "What do you think happened to Anita?"

"I don't know."

"Do you know what happened to Harrady?"

"Someone said he was teaching at a school in Norfolk."

"As in Virginia?"

He nodded.

"And he's deaf?" I asked, my frown growing.

Deaf people must get tired of the ignorance of the hearing. "Yeah," he said. "Call him."

My face asked how.

"All you need is a TTY or TDD—a telephone typewriter or a telecommunications device for the deaf. That really just means a phone and a keyboard—unless you have the computer model. TDD's are similar to modems. You type over the telephone line instead of talk."

"And what do you do if you don't happen to have one of those machines?"

"Use a relay service. In metropolitan areas the deaf communities supply them. You call in, and the middleman with a TDD sends your message. Even the telephone companies are getting in the act now. They're supplying conversations. They type the message to the deaf and orally pass it on to the hearing."

"You talked to Anita with a TDD?"

"Yes."

"Do the TDD's have printouts?"

"Most of them. Mine does."

"Did you keep any of Anita's messages?"

He shook his head.

"And I could call you over a TDD if I had any further questions?"

"If you had my number."

He took one of the four pens out of his front pocket and wrote his number for me. "I hope you find her," he said.

He was a smart young man who still knew how to love. I envied him a little bit, but not too much.

5

THE BRAGGING RIGHTS TO being closest to heaven in San Francisco fall between the Bank of America World Headquarters Building and the Transamerica Pyramid. For once the pharaohs beat the prophets, or profits, as the spire of the pyramid noses out the moneychangers by seventy-four feet.

Small change? San Francisco isn't Manhattan and never wants to be. We'll take Victorian, thank you, and hold the seventy stories. In most parts of San Francisco you're aware there is a sky. North Beach, Chinatown, even Nob Hill—all are free from high-rises. It's only around Montgomery Street, twelve blocks of skyscrapers, where Goliath rules. While entering the City on 101, I looked at the skyline and made an association new to me—from a distance the buildings looked like gravestones, with the epitaphs written in the spaced windows. It wasn't the most cheery thought to head for a drink on.

I parked and then walked up Kearny to get to the B of A Building. Every city has its insider jokes, and the Bank of America unwittingly provided one. It commissioned a sculpture by a Japanese artist, 200 tons of black granite that stand fourteen feet high. I don't know the official title of the piece, I don't think anyone knows, but San Franciscans call it "The Banker's Heart." I hadn't eaten lunch, so I didn't worry about losing it on the high-speed elevator ride to the Carnelian Room on the fifty-second floor. The

Room is plush, but people remember the view—about the best in the City—over the decor. I got off the elevator, hat and stomach in hand, and found Leland waiting.

"Hi, handsome," he said.

He was carrying my requested books and magazines, and as I relieved him of them I replied, "Can it, Lee."

Lee isn't really a flamer, but whenever we go out together he invariably exaggerates his propensities. I wondered if being in the company of a straight threatened his homosexuality, and if he compensated in much the same way male heterosexuals out-macho themselves when a homosexual is around. I found his public behavior amusing sometimes, offensive at others. My patience vanished as he did his version of the shimmy while we were being led to our seats.

"Quit swishing," I whispered.

"I thought you'd never notice," he said in a voice not quite a whisper.

His gyrations stopped when he sat down. The sun was falling and Baghdad by the Bay was going grey. She was a marvelous creature in shadows, artful with her makeup and beguiling. Lee and I were easily caught up in her spell, and watched her for a few minutes without words.

A human voice interrupted. I was slow to look up, but the waitress was almost pretty enough to make me forgive her intrusion. She was amused by my reverie, and we smiled for each other. Lee decided he didn't like our body language. His hand lightly touched mine, and his motion was a stroking one. His words sounded even more suggestive than his gesture.

"Why don't you order for us, darling?"

I took my hand out of patting range. "Glenfiddich neat for me, and a pink lady for my acquaintance."

"Make that a vodka and tonic," said Lee pettishly.

The waitress was amused. She touched me playfully on the shoulder while walking by. I surreptitiously admired her black-stockinged legs as she passed, until Lee's head somehow blocked my vision.

"How's your ex-wife?" he asked innocently.

"I wouldn't know."

"She was in the *Examiner* the other day. Something about a horse event."

"That sounds like Paula."

"Nothing like a good mount, I guess."

My eyes cautioned him.

"She married again, didn't she?"

"At least once."

"And what does he do?"

"What I did. Once."

"You don't like to talk about that. You never gave me more than bits and pieces."

"That's all I was. Bits and pieces."

"You were prettier then," he said, "but didn't have the character, the strength in looks and bearing, you have now. I noticed you immediately. So well built, so tall, so beautiful. But lost. Very, very lost. I saw your grey eyes looking all around. I decided you were a young man I wanted to help."

"Wanted to seduce."

"That too," said Lee phlegmatically. "But I don't think you knew that when I approached you, and asked if you needed help finding anything. You told me you were just looking for something good to read."

"I'm surprised you didn't recommend the latest issue of *The Advocate.*"

"Do you remember our little tour?" Lee asked proudly. "That was ten years ago."

"I remember," I said.

Paula and I had met in college. We talked about justice, and peace, and working toward a better world, but mostly we made love. We waxed poetic on literature like all good lit majors are supposed to, and when the courses were finished we enrolled in Real Life 101. We were married, and I began work at her father's company. He was a director of one of the big investment houses in one of the big buildings on Montgomery Street, the so-called Wall Street of the west. The area's financial roots go back to gold-rush days, when Montgomery Street was an unpaved expanse of dirt. No limos then, no fifty-thousand-dollar cars parked in garages that charge fifty dollars a day. Mules were the preferred transportation, because whenever it rained Montgomery Street became a wide quagmire. A hard deluge sometimes resulted in a sign that read, "This street is impassible. Not even jackassable."

I might have preferred hustling my claim with jeans and a pickax, but I came to work with a three-piece suit and a briefcase. My father-in-law pulled some heavy strings and got me into the Pacific Union Club, and all the while I worked on becoming respectable. I never realized how much it took to become respectable.

Most people with brains won't argue with the good life. I was twenty-six, and probably just finishing up with puberty, when the brain damage first showed its symptoms. Paula and I had been married for four years. We lived in a four-bedroom house in Sausalito, courtesy of daddy, and my tennis game was better than ever. I could talk tax deferments, portfolio strategies, and return on investments with the best of them. We had a rose garden, and I slept at night like a baby.

No one ever told me about thorns and nightly changings.

When I first noticed our firm was doing some very wrong, some very unethical things, I could have turned my head, but I didn't. I decided to bray a little. I went to my father-in-law and told him of my suspicions. I spoke about Securities and Exchange Commission violations, about the possibility of outside audits and investigations. And I was politely, avuncularly even, told not to worry, that my matters of concern would be looked into.

First you speak soothingly to a jackass.

The weeks went by and my suspicions increased. I started asking a few questions around the office, and I didn't get any answers that made me feel better. So I told Paula about my dilemma, and she told me to shelve my worries. Her daddy, and her daddy's firm, were not crooks. Sometimes you had to cut corners in business, didn't I know that? And wasn't daddy treating us well?

Then you try stroking a jackass.

But I was naive. I thought I could root out the evil and make the office and the world a little better. So with a kick of my hind legs I went on the hunt. I made some inquiries, did a little nosing around, and began to smell some of the manure in the pasture. And then I was called into his office.

My father-in-law wanted to know why I was bothering some of his key people. And how was it that I had time for matters other than my job? He assured me, in no uncertain terms, that the firm could and was doing its own in-house investigation, and that my efforts were detrimental. And embarrassing. And would not be tolerated.

Then you speak loudly to a jackass, threaten it.

I let some days pass, which turned into weeks, and outwardly I acquiesced, but I never stopped thinking. After a while I did more than think. And the strange thing was I liked it—liked being able to figure out how to follow a trail, and how to read as much into situations where information was suppressed as where everything was spelled out. I started working late hours, ostensibly on a merger, but it was my first case. And I solved it, but I learned that's a far different thing from being successful.

I documented insider information being bought and sold. I substantiated collusion and kickbacks, and a score of other infractions that could potentially shut the firm down. And late one night I left all of my findings on the desk of Paula's father.

And when the jackass won't move, you hit it on the head with a shovel. If you don't kill it, the jackass will move.

I was fired the next morning.

And just when the jackass was staggering, the second blow of the day came. Paula served me with divorce papers. They cited mental cruelty, but I think Paula realized I was getting to be too good an investigator. I began to question her equestrian outings, began to wonder who her mount really was. I had seen the loose threads at the office, and then seen them at home. A telephone number here, a diaphragm missing there.

A suspicious mind is bad enough. Confirmation is worse. Yes, Montgomery Street is jackassable. Life is jackassable. But sometimes there's not a hell of a lot to hee-haw about.

"You took home all the books I recommended," said Lee. "Every one."

"It was interesting learning about San Francisco's history."

I listened to myself mouth an understatement. San Francisco's history had more than interested me. It might have saved my life. At the least it made me notice things again. Everywhere I walked in the City, everywhere I turned, I found the lives and dreams and follies of others. There's a continuity and reassurance to history. It both humbles and elevates. Knowing the past gives you a wider vision. You get a feel for those bricks under your feet, and the hands that placed them there.

"Every day you came for another book."

"My docket wasn't exactly full."

"And I could see you were getting better, getting that look back in your eyes. That mulish look."

"Jackassable."

"What's the difference?"

"Mules are sterile."

"I didn't exactly see you painting the town red."

I drank my Scotch and agreed in silence. It hadn't been a good time. Goethe once said, "Know thyself? If I knew myself, I'd run away." But I'd taken that hard look inside, and decided what I could live with, and what I couldn't. I decided to be clean. Norman's words were still in my head: "Cleanliness is next to godliness." It sounded priggish, but maybe there was some truth in it.

"It didn't take you that long to get better. Maybe a month. I knew you were okay when you presented me with that fake medal."

I had made a copy of a Carnegie Medal on display in Special Collections. It had been awarded to a man who aided fellow workers overcome by sewer gas. Maybe I knew what it was like to be overcome by sewer gas.

"I thought you deserved a medal."

"Which I still proudly display above my desk. But when you announced what you were going to do for a living, I wondered if you were really all right."

"I wondered, too."

"I mean, who really is a private detective these days?"

"You accused me of trying to be a stereotype."

"I did. The glib, rugged-looking man going out to solve crime. I told you to keep your fantasies in the bedroom."

"You were a little more graphic than that."

"I didn't think you'd stick it out."

"I tested the water first, if you remember. Did my six thousand hours of intern gumshoeing. Didn't even buy a gun until after my license was framed."

"What's this case about?" he asked.

"A missing deaf woman."

"What?" Lee exaggerated loudly. I didn't bite.

"Do you want to go for some dim sum?" I asked.

"No," said Lee. He looked a little ashamed. "Joe said he was cooking a special dish. I think he called it the Native Son Surprise, or something like that."

I smiled. "He does know I'm straight, doesn't he?"

"Yes. But he's not comfortable with you."

"I think homosexuals are more prejudiced than heterosexuals."

Five years previously I would have said, "I think queers are more prejudiced than normal people."

"There might be something to that," said Lee.

"Native Son Surprise, huh?" It reminded me of something.

Lee nodded.

I cleared my throat for a recital:

> *"The Miners came in '49,*
> *The Whores in '51,*
> *And when they got together,*
> *They produced the native son."*

Lee smiled. He remembered the rhyme. But Lee was originally from Connecticut. I was the native Californian. I was the native son.

6

I SPENT THE MORNING in my office writing up observations and making calls. I had neglected putting my notes in order, and tried gathering all of my jottings into something resembling a report. With enough organized observations in front of you, sometimes a dim light goes on in your head, and sometimes you even realize you've made your case. I never carried a tape recorder. It was more than people freezing in the presence of a machine, more than the hassles of transcribing those tapes. Opposing attorneys know only too well that they can ask for your tape recordings, tapes that can sometimes be detrimental to your case. But they don't have a right to reports or observations unless they're in the form of signed statements, something I don't ask for. In legal jargon my reports were "not discoverable." I liked being not discoverable.

The phone rang and I was suddenly discovered.

"Don't you believe in calling your answering service?"

"Miss Tuntland, I know you've heard this before, but I was just going to call."

"If I wasn't wearing chocolate lipstick and staring at a dozen beautiful roses, I wouldn't believe you. As it is, I just have my doubts."

"Treats and sweets for a fair maiden," I extolled.

"Tinsel boodle for your pet poodle," Miss Tuntland pooh-poohed, but pleasantly pooh-poohed. "But before the chocolate cloys in my mouth I better pass on your information. Mrs. Walters, remember her, the one with the voice, wants you to call her this morning. I also made your appointment at the Gorilla Project for tomorrow morning at eleven. Your contact is Dr. William Harrison, no relation to the general I'm sure, but autocratic nonetheless. He was less than pleased to spare the time for you so I wouldn't count on a welcome mat. The address is 1211 Overhill Road."

I wrote down the address and heeded her warning. Miss Tuntland's impressions were invariably right.

"I also turned down more business for you yesterday. The uninteresting but highly profitable cases that you seem to eschew."

"Thank you?" I answered.

"Have you called Denise yet?"

"I did. She gave me a week's reprieve." The fact of life for private detectives is that in order to make a living you usually have to work on about ten cases at a time. It was unusual that I was devoting all of my attention to one case. Miss Tuntland seemed to know that better than I.

As we said our good-byes, I hung up the phone and thought some dangerous thoughts: someday I'd visit that woman, someday I'd bring the roses in person. I think we were both scared of that day.

I dialed Tammy Walters's number. After identifying myself, and getting just a touch of her over-the-wire charm school voice, I heard the expectant pause. "Nothing substantial yet, Mrs. Walters."

I didn't allow time for the usual disappointed pause. "Did you arrange a time for me to talk with your husband?"

"I did, though he was very reluctant. He was never happy about me hiring a private detective."

"When and where will we meet?"

"The Standard Oil Building on Bush Street. His office

is on the eighth floor. He said he would be free tomorrow at four."

"I'll be there. Will you be free, also?"

"Unfortunately not."

"Then I'll ask you a few questions now. Does the name Will Harrady mean anything to you?"

"I don't think so."

"What about Darren Fielder?"

"He's one of Anita's friends."

"Did she speak of him much?"

"No."

"Did you get acquainted with any of the friends Anita made while she was living in her Russian Hill apartment?"

"No."

"Did she ever mention their names?"

"No."

"I understand she was a model for a group of artists. Did she talk about that with you?"

"Not that I remember."

"Do you have her TDD at your house?"

"Yes."

"And does it have a printer?"

"Yes."

"Did you notice whether she kept any printouts?"

"I don't think there are any. The police went through all her belongings. They looked at everything from her apartment."

"But you haven't thrown anything out?"

"No."

"One last question: Did you ever hear the name Kevin Bateson?"

"That's Anita's photographer friend."

"Do you have his number or address?"

"He has a photographic studio with his name. I understand he's now in Tiburon."

I asked for the address of Anita's old apartment in Rus-

sian Hill, and also took down the Walterses' Piedmont
address.

"I'd like to talk with you further," I said, "and I'll also
need to search through Anita's belongings."

"Fine," she said, then remembered. "Tuesdays and
Thursdays are bridge days."

I refrained from saying that missing daughters ranked
above trump cards.

There are worse things than driving to Tiburon on a
sunny day. I crossed over the Golden Gate Bridge. In 1846
explorer John C. Fremont compared the strait the bridge
spans to Constantinople's Golden Horn and thus it was
christened. In modern times the price of real estate brought
even greater truth to the naming.

I stopped for lunch along with half of San Francisco at
Sam's Anchor Cafe. Like all of Tiburon's restaurants,
Sam's sits on the waterfront. If its food and drinks will
never get it a star in Michelin, its view and relaxed atmosphere ought to. I unbuttoned a few shirt buttons, ordered
a sandwich, and asked for a double Scotch. For a little
while I pretended I was again one of the gentry. I was a
single among deuces and four-tops, and my status rele-
gated me to a chair next to the rope-enclosed deck, a fate
I didn't bemoan, for it got me a little further from the
Marin talk and a little closer to the brine.

It was a day for the Bay, and if I couldn't scan all 450
square miles of it, I wasn't shortchanged by much. Angel
Island appeared touchable, and paradise never looked so
close. Saint Francis was only six miles across the water,
which made for a double ecclesiastic dosing. The only
fault I could find in the day was that my sandwich was
slow in arriving. It was probably my fault for having ordered a deviled ham.

Tiburon is touristy. There's not much to it besides the
traps you'd expect. Kevin Bateson's studio was on Bridge-

way, the main street. It was nestled between two prefab
ye-olde kind of stores that even A. A. Milne wouldn't
have gushed over. I parked near a pink scripted sign that
read Bateson Photographic Studio. When I opened the
door I was greeted by bells clanging. But cutely clanging.

A blonde appeared and smiled on cue. She was cute,
and her figure was ripe. Maybe too ripe. She was three
cup sizes removed from *Vogue*. I was tempted to raise an
imaginary camera and say cheese. Or maybe cheesecake.

"May I help you?"

"I'd like to see Kevin Bateson."

"I'm sorry, he's doing a shoot right now."

"That's okay. I always wanted to see one."

I walked around her butt, and her "but, buts," past all
the artfully decorated wedding pictures and graduation
shots and octogenarians smiling after fifty years of nuptial
bliss. I paused only at a cold-cream ad, and Anita Walters
bending her face to the softness of the product. The blonde
caught up with me there, but I walked by her again toward
the sounds in the back.

"Kevin . . . Mr. Bateson, I told him . . ."

Bateson and his model turned and stared at me. "Go
ahead," I said benevolently. "I'm a friend of a friend here
to see Kevin. I just thought I'd watch him at work."

The model looked at Bateson uncertainly, and Bateson
gave me the same look. He must have decided it would be
too much trouble getting rid of me.

"Okay," he said, and then a little louder, "Okay."

The blonde disappeared, and Bateson repositioned the
model. They were working on a set with a white backdrop.
It was clear the woman wasn't a professional, a decision I
didn't base entirely on her face and figure. The camera
tells a different story than the human eye, but it was more
than that. The woman was inexperienced. Bateson walked
her through shots and wardrobe. She was pretty, but he

was prettier. He was young, early thirties, and as slick as his dark, greased back hair.

"Beautiful," "great," "that's it," "hold it," "wonderful," "give me that smile," "that's a winner," and "ooooh heartbreaker" were a good part of his shooting vocabulary. He had endless film and patience, and what seemed to me good technique. He didn't mind constantly positioning the model, and his coaching wasn't all verbal. He worked with his hands, and lingered with them also. The model didn't complain.

"That's a wrap, Vicky," he finally said, and added a little more Hollywood by giving her a hug and a kiss. "I'll have the portfolio ready for you next Thursday. Why don't you change and see Angela up front for details."

There was another theatrical hug and then Vicky disappeared. Bateson pretended that he had forgotten about me while he rolled up some film.

"How much?" My voice echoed a little on the backdrop. He looked up at me from his camera and pretended again. This time that he didn't understand.

"Huh?"

"How much is she paying you for the session? To pretend that she has what it takes to be a model?"

"I don't like the tone of your voice."

"Let me guess. A Marin housewife. And all of her friends have always said, 'Vicky, you should be a model.' "

My echo was getting a little louder. "We'd better talk in my office," he said hurriedly.

I followed him. And I found Anita Walters. In eight-by-tens, and a few more ads, and a couple of color shots. She was the only model featured on the walls in his office. I took my time examining her.

"What do you want?"

"You still haven't answered my question."

"Four hundred, but that's for two portfolios, hers and mine."

"And let me guess again, you have access to top agents, and they're always going through your portfolios?"

Bateson proved he could still blush. "What do you want?" he asked again.

I gave him my card and pointed to a picture of Anita. She was leaning against a tree, her knees drawn forward to her body, a pensive beauty.

"I'm investigating the disappearance of Anita Walters."

Bateson gave me a little pout, but didn't say anything. I tried to encourage his mouth along.

"Where did you meet Anita?" I asked.

"I literally ran into her on the street."

"And you said, 'How would you like to be a model?' "

"I said it with much more savoir faire."

"It didn't faze you that she was deaf?"

"Not in the least."

"I understand you two had a fight while she was still at Greenmont."

I felt him tense, even if he tried not to show it. "Who said that?"

His was a very good question, since no one had. "I understand because of your fight Anita didn't allow you to photograph her during her last year of school."

"I photographed her."

His denial wasn't strong enough, so I let the silence mount.

"I photographed her a few times."

"So where is she now?"

"I don't know. At first I thought she was purposely being mysterious, you know, just disappearing . . ."

"But now you think she's dead?"

The word came reluctantly out of his mouth. "Yes."

"Why?"

"If she was trying to get back at us, this wouldn't be Anita's way. She liked active retaliation."

"You sound like you know."

He decided to give me his honest look, his "let's get it all off my chest" attitude. It didn't make me like him any better.

"I do," he said. "You're mostly right about her not letting me shoot her during her last years at Greenmont. I discovered her. I guess I loved her. And then we did have a fight. And after that, the few times she'd let me see her, the few times she'd let me photograph her, were more active teasing than anything else."

"What was the fight about?"

"I'd rather not say."

He looked ready to pout again, so I decided not to press it.

"You said she teased you after your fight. How did she do that?"

"It's hard to describe. If I tell you it was mostly looks and glances, you'll probably say I imagined it. But she knew how to jab both personally and professionally. She showed me letters from other modeling agencies, and made sure others told me about her work as an art model."

"Who did she work for?"

"I never asked their names."

"Were you lovers?"

"No."

My eyebrows spoke for me.

"She wasn't interested."

I thought about that. It gave me a more positive opinion of Anita. "May I see her portfolio?" I asked.

He swiveled his chair and opened a file cabinet. I saw him carefully separate some binders, and then he handed me a folder. I thumbed through the photos for a few minutes, and separated some duplicates. I couldn't swear I did it for professional reasons. Usually I'm dispassionate about photos of beautiful women. Imperfect flesh has always seemed a far better thing than a perfect glossy. But I made my request.

"May I have these?"

Kevin Bateson nodded. His blonde came and interrupted our chat. "Mrs. Hutton is here for her session."

"I have more questions," I said.

"Why don't you call for an appointment next time?"

His question was pertinent, and his spunk was returning, so I decided it was a good time to leave. I said my thanks, and then walked out of the studio, hardly pausing to eye Mrs. Hutton and her slinky bathing suit.

"All right, Greta, great. Good. That's it. Make love to the camera, come, make love to the camera."

Whatever happened to good old, "Say cheese," I wondered.

7

TOO OFTEN PAY PHONES sport a view of crumbled asphalt and broken glass, or advertised beer specials posted in the windows of some convenience store. The good thing about Tiburon is that they have a few pay phones that look out to the Bay. Plunk your quarters and chat to the panoramic expanse. Which is what I did.

The gulls were active. I identified several varieties without the help of binoculars. People tend to think all gulls are the same, but among the subfamily Laridae there are a lot of physical and behavioral differences. Unfortunately, raucous and mewing cries are one universal gull trait, and the chorus was in full swing. There were Western gulls, Heermann's gulls, and some immature Herring gulls. Background music might have also been supplied by a Thayer gull or two, and maybe a Glaucous-winged gull, but I couldn't be sure. The birds were swooping down on the pleasure crafts and accepting the offerings.

They're interesting birds, but not my favorite ornithological study. They remind me too much of humans. I once witnessed two monied jokers throwing their loose change around in the Bowery. The laughter of the exhibition makers was worse than the curses of the scuttling and jostling derelicts. Their laughter reminded me of the grating cries of the gulls. I still remembered their laughter even though I hadn't let it last for long.

"I have your caller now."

I conveyed my message and request, and the operator repeated my words back to me for approval. I wondered if young deaf lovers used this service, wondered if impassioned "I love you's" were mouthed and then relayed through unenthusiastic middlemen. The operator passed on my message, and told me in turn that Ellen expected me at seven, and promised to have Will Harrady's number waiting. Her closing remark "looking forward to seeing you" didn't sound right or exciting out of proxy lips, but I reminded myself it shouldn't have, anyway.

With a few hours to spare I decided to look up Anita's old apartment. Russian Hill has always prided itself on its eclectic neighborhoods. The rich and the bohemian have historically lived side by side, even if today there are far more of the former and far fewer of the latter. Lombard Street, which advertises itself as "the crookedest street in the world," is in Russian Hill, a street where every movie chase scene in the world has managed to get filmed.

There are several stories behind the naming of Russian Hill. I liked a few of them, and those I didn't I discounted. Some said a colony of Russians had settled on the 360-foot summit, while others said a group of Russian sailors had been buried there. Whatever, the name had stuck. The artists and writers had called it home—the poet Sterling, the satirist Bierce—but the spirit of the place had been in the William Penn Humphries house, now long gone. When the house was threatened by fire in 1906 and no water was available to stem the flames, its owner had challenged the conflagration with champagne. Smoking woodwork was doused with quarts and magnums of Mumm's and Crug's Private Cuvee. I don't know if toasts were called or prayers made, but the flames retreated.

Anita's apartment was near where the Humphries Castle had once stood. It also wasn't far from where the gallows for the first official execution in San Francisco were erected.

I found Anita's building, and buzzed long enough to get the manager's attention. It was clear I wasn't the first person to ask him about Anita. The man's name was Rizzo. He talked to me through the security door.

"Huh, what can I tell you? I been through this before, three, four times. I don't know nothin'. Okay?"

"Then how about letting me in so I can talk to her neighbors?"

"Hey! This is a security buildin', can't you see? I let you in, it's not secure, get it?"

"Then maybe you can answer a few questions."

"Hey! You're not listenin'. I don't know nothin'."

It was clear my golden tongue wasn't going to get me inside, or keep him there much longer. I waved Andrew Jackson, and found the key to the door.

"I really don't know nothin'," said Rizzo, this time face to face, and Jackson already interred in his pocket. "I said hello a few times. She was a real looker, you know."

"What about her friends?"

"Why should I see them? They buzz her, she buzzes back, they're in."

"She was deaf, though."

"She had some kind of contraption hooked to a light when somebody buzzed."

"But she still wouldn't have known who was downstairs."

"All the apartments got deadbolts and peepholes. She don't want someone in her place, they don't get in."

"Do you live here?"

"Yeah."

"Do you handle noise complaints?"

"What few there are. We don't got rowdies here."

"Anita Walters had some parties in her place. Did you ever have to caution her?"

"No."

"Were you ever in her apartment before her disappearance?"

"Once."

"Why?"

"I do repairs here. I do goddamn everything."

"And what kind of a repair did she need?"

"She needed a couple of things. I don't remember."

"Do you keep a log?"

"Yeah. And do you want to fix the commode in 462 while I look it up?"

I added another dead president, Lincoln, to gain his goodwill. By his expression he would have preferred Alexander Hamilton, and hold the first office.

"I'll look it up." He started to leave.

"Who's the best neighbor to talk to?"

"Old lady Houston. Mrs. Houston. In 301. Been here forever and lives at her peephole. Gave the cops plenty of theories on that babe's disappearance. Would've solved the Lindbergh kidnapping and Kennedy shooting if they had asked.

"And Lincoln's," he added somewhat disdainfully, before disappearing around a corner.

If Mrs. Houston wasn't perched at her keyhole, she wasn't far from it. Her voice was only a beat behind my knock. I announced myself, and upon request dutifully produced identification. The door opened slowly and I was ushered in.

The apartment was well furnished, mainly with antiques. The air smelled as old as the furniture. I trudged through its mustiness while being led to a chair.

It took some effort for Mrs. Houston to get seated, but her mind didn't need the extra moments her body did. "I wondered why no one had come back," she said, "but then the police didn't seem too interested in my opinions."

"And which opinions are those, Mrs. Houston?"

She pursed her lips and thought. She was an old woman

who did not want to be excited or frightened by Anita's disappearance, but she was both. She wasn't confused, but it was important to her that she speak her thoughts clearly. She was neither crackpot nor eccentric, not feisty or senile, just a person who had lived more years than most. It was clear she remembered the past, maybe too well.

"I told the police that they should question her acquaintances as to her whereabouts."

It was a logical enough statement, and one that begged for a little more prying. Mrs. Houston needed to know that I was interested in what she had to say, and not just another in a long like of skeptics. "I am trying to track down her acquaintances," I said, using her word. "Can you tell me about them?"

"I can." She suddenly covered her mouth in alarm. "I should have offered you something to drink, Mr. Winter."

Normally a private investigator accepts any offer. A drink in hand means you can nurse a conversation for an extra five minutes. But in this instance staying wouldn't be the problem. Getting away might be. "I'm fine, thanks."

"Maybe I am getting forgetful," she said regretfully. "Imagine, not offering you tea. And imagine that at first I didn't even notice she was deaf. I don't know why. Maybe because she was so pretty. A lot of things get overlooked if you're pretty. Or rich."

I smiled, already liking her. She was three for three in declarative statements.

"And despite what Mr. Rizzo might have told you, Mr. Winter, I am quite content to let other people lead their lives without my interference. But I did take special notice of Anita, even if I didn't know her."

"Why?"

"I think the lonely-old-lady part is the smaller consideration," she said with dignity. "I think anyone would have become interested in Anita. My patio window looks into her unit. Anita must have liked natural light. She never closed the curtains. Never. And because of that I noticed her flashing lights. It took me a while to figure them out. To figure her out. But I did."

There was some pride in her voice.

"I watched her from my dining room table. I'd sit and drink tea. I don't think she ever noticed me. Old people are like chameleons. We blend in. Not like her friends."

"Tell me about her friends."

"They looked like beatniks."

I hid my smile. I hadn't heard that word in twenty years. "Was there a regular group?"

"A few. But there were always new faces."

"Were they noisy?"

"No. When they came over it wasn't a Quaker meeting, but I can remember having louder tea parties. I think they respected Anita that way. But I would rather they had been talkative."

"Why?"

"They were strange. And not just from an old woman's perspective."

"In what way?"

"I think I'd like some tea. Are you sure?"

I declined her pouring motion with a spread of my level hand. Maybe these books I was reading were right. Maybe most of our communication is without words. Mrs. Houston got her tea, and we moved to her viewing table. The drapes to Anita's old apartment were now closed.

"They put on shows." Mrs. Houston tasted her tea, and made a twisted face. I couldn't be sure if it was from a memory or the tea.

"What kind of shows?"

She answered slowly. "Strange things. Hard to describe."

"Try."

"They were never the same. They used candles, and lights, and machines that projected pictures, sometimes awful pictures. There was artwork. Sometimes they even wore masks."

"Was everybody involved?"

"No. Usually no more than three people."

"And how large was the audience?"

"Ten people or so. Our apartments aren't that large."

"How frequent were these performances?"

"Once or twice a month."

"How many did you witness?"

"Maybe six."

"The same performers?"

"No."

I mulled the information over. "What about sound? Did they have tapes or music?"

"Yes, but it was kept at a very low level."

"How long did these plays last?"

"Usually not more than ten minutes."

The data still wasn't computing. "Were these shows directed toward any one individual?"

"I think two. Anita and a man I heard others call Vincent."

"Tell me about him."

"A big man, as tall as you, I think. And he always wore black. Always."

"He was there for all the performances?"

"Yes."

"Describe him further."

"He had a thick beard. I don't like beards. You can never read a bearded face."

"Any other physical characteristics?"

"None that I remember. Or care to."

"Was Vincent ever over by himself?"

"Not that I saw."

"Did Anita entertain any other men alone?"

"Not that I noticed."

"Did she often have visitors?"

"Not often. Maybe once a week."

"Did you ever notice any deaf people?"

"Only a few."

"Can you describe them?"

She looked embarrassed. "I can't. I think mostly I watched their hands. They looked pretty to me. Their hands, that is."

"What kind of hours did Anita keep?"

"Odd hours. She was in and out. Usually she was up and out before I awakened."

"Did she always sleep in her apartment?"

"It seemed that way."

"Did you hear any other names? Can you describe the people with them?"

"There was a dark-haired woman, big, that is, well developed. She didn't wear a brassiere most of the time. She was one of the performers. And they called her Goldilocks. I couldn't figure out why."

"Anyone else?"

"No, I'm sorry." Mrs. Houston finished her tea. We both stared at Anita's apartment for a while. I wondered if it was only drapes she had left open. Maybe someone could have entered through her patio doors. It would have taken some gymnastics, but wouldn't have called for a gold medal winner. Just another psycho.

"Anita is thought to have disappeared on New Year's Eve. Did you notice anything unusual about that time?"

"No."

"You never saw her upset? Never saw her fight with anyone?"

She shook her head.

I got up. It was a tired get-up. "Are you in the telephone book, Mrs. Houston? I might have some follow-up questions."

"I'm listed. But don't be afraid just to stop by. And if you find her, do tell me."

"I will."

"You must think me an awful snoop," she said. "I'm ashamed I know as much as I do. But she was so pretty and unusual. I never even said hello to her in person. I wish I had done that."

I almost said, "Maybe you will," but settled instead on a smile and a few comforting words. I gave her my card at the door, then heard the deadbolt behind me.

I buzzed Rizzo for the third time, but he didn't answer. I remembered the commode in 462 and rang there.

"Mrs. Curtin ain't here."

"Mr. Winter is."

Rizzo grumbled something, and then I heard pages flip over the intercom. "December twenty-eighth. Busted sink faucet. And broken cabinet. I credited her for the faucet. Charged her for the cabinet."

"What happened?"

"I never asked."

"What about a guess?"

"I ain't good at guessing."

"So describe your repairs."

"The faucets are a bunch of crap. We've got the kind where there's a long thinnish handle. You move it along towards hot and cold. Up gets you the water, down it's off."

"And the handle was broken off?"

"Right."

"How long was the handle?"

"Six inches or so."

"Have other people broken them?"

"I've seen the hell bent out of them."

"But not broken?"

"No. I figured this was the first. Won't be the last."

"And the cabinet?"

"It was wrenched off its hinges."

"Are they well secured?"

"I couldn't pull one off."

"Thanks."

I still had a little time, and decided I'd rather kill it in San Francisco than Oakland. I drove over to Norman's professional building on Van Ness, and by pretending I was one of his patients was allowed to park. Validation would probably mean giving up another theory to Norman.

I found him between patients. He was dictating into a machine, hard at work on another one of his pop psychology books. I think his last one was cutely titled *Rainbows From Blues.* He never adequately answered whether there as a golden chamber pot at the end of his supposed rainbows.

Norman never liked his genius interrupted, but he stopped his dictating when I walked into his office. I suspected he didn't do it out of politeness, but rather fear of my commentary. I found my place on his couch and kicked off my shoes. "A trim," I said, "light around the sides."

"One of us is working, Mr. Clean."

I ignored the name. "Both of us are. I need your expertise in the arts. I needed a cognoscente."

Norman stroked his beard. That was his equivalent to a purr. But he did know his stuff.

"I'm not too familiar with performance art," I said, "but I think that's what I'm dealing with. You're versed in what's going on?"

"Quite."

"Does the name Goldilocks ring a bell?"

I expected some remark about the three bears, but Norman was serious about his art. "Goldilocks is a very talented performer."

"What's she doing now?"

"She's working on a new production scheduled to open in a few weeks. It's going to be performed at the Masonic

Temple. Better call well ahead for your tickets, and demand center seating."

"Did you ever meet Goldilocks in any of your gadfly
functions?"

"No. But I saw her in both *Feathered Flesh* and *I Once
Owned A Dog With Three Legs*. She was excellent in
both."

"I missed those," I said, successfully without sarcasm.
"Tell me about her and them."

"She's a striking woman, and so are her pieces. In
Feathered Flesh she plays Raca, a woman in a cage, in a
cage, in a cage. She wanted to become a phoenix, wanted
to burn and be reborn from the ashes and finally fly."

"And did she?"

"Yes, but her resurrection didn't mean the disappearance
of all the cages. Her rebirth was magical and then tragic.
I don't think I'll ever forget her scream at the end. Imagine
being given a miracle, and then facing the mockery of another cage. It was the essence of betrayals."

"So she played a cagey character?"

"God. My patients would sue me for malpractice if I
punned like that. And if I had to analyze your puerile so-
called wit . . ."

"Don't. Tell me about another name: Vincent."

"I'm surprised you haven't heard of him. He's the hot-
test name in art right now. And he also happens to be the
director of the upcoming play at the Masonic Temple."

"So he's a director?"

"No, that's a first for him. He's an artist."

"As in canvases?"

"That and other material. I understand he's designed a
lot of the sets. I'm sure he'll make more money from selling them than the play will take in."

"Is he of any school?"

"No. Which I guess means he's Post-modern. His works

are very bold, very graphic. Sometimes macabre. They don't appeal to the senses—they challenge them."

I made some notes. I don't think shrinks are comfortable on the other end of a jotting pencil. Norman fidgeted.

"Interesting case?"

"Yes," I said. "Missing young lady. Deaf. With a lot of hear-no-evil acquaintances."

"I'd like to hear more."

"Saturday night at the Castle? Ten o'clock?"

"I'll be there."

"Leave your couch at the office."

I gauged my time, and decided to swing by the Masonic Temple in the hope that rehearsals would be going on. The Temple is located at 1111 California. I had never been inside, but was able to gain entry when the door sentry went off on some task. My expectations of an intimate setting were quickly dashed. The auditorium contained about 3000 more seats than Anita's apartment. I wandered down the far left aisle toward the thrust stage. All the players were huddled on the sidelines watching a large, bearded man I assumed was Vincent. He commanded the stage with his brooding posture. Periodically he waved his arms in exaggerated gestures, and stagehands scurried to move the sets to his bidding. His black outfit seemed to match his mood.

But there was someone else who interested me more, a woman who had to be Goldilocks. She was large and dark, coiffed with raven spikes and masked with a lot of pancake makeup. Her languid posture and insouciant expression contrasted with those of the other figures, which looked huddled and fearful. She wanted everyone to know she was bored.

Goldilocks had on a flower print dress, with a potato bag top. Idaho would have been proud to lay claim to the harvest. She looked approachable, so I approached. I liked the fact that she didn't pretend I wasn't there. She searched me with dark eyes that managed to look intelligent even with red eyeliner.

"Did you bring a drink?" she asked.

"Do you need one?"

"Why else would I have asked?"

"Maybe you wanted to take advantage of me."

She laughed, but not too mockingly, and then surveyed me a second time. "I've had worse ideas." Her tone wasn't too insulting either.

"How about we go for a drink, then?"

"I can't. I have to wait for Vincent to stop jerking off."

"How long does that usually take?"

"Ten, fifteen minutes."

"You've got time for some masturbatis interruptus, then. Let's get a drink."

She debated for the length of her smile, then grabbed my hand and led us out through a side door. "There's a place nearby," she said. "They're beginning to know me there."

"I wonder why."

She tilted one of her spiked hair balls at me, and proceeded to gore my shoulder. In the light of day she looked to be about thirty, though her assorted baubles and combined styles gave her a younger look. "Who are you?"

"How many people have said 'Papa Bear'?"

"About a thousand jerks."

"Stuart Winter. Private investigator."

"You're kidding."

"No."

"God. I always wanted to meet a private dick. I mean, in the flesh."

"But flesh is weak," I said.

"And don't I love it," she said, then added, "Are you carrying a piece?"

I wasn't sure of her reference. "I don't have a gun, no," I said.

She turned to me, ran her hands up and down my chest, and said, "Then you don't mind if I frisk you."

I was debating an answer, when she turned again, this time into a bar. San Francisco has 1,500 of them, three bars for every church. I've always thought that if churches sold communion wine they'd do a better Sunday business. Goldilocks didn't order cream and porridge. She had a Tanqueray double with a splash of tonic.

"So what kind of case are you on?"

"The disappearance of Anita Walters."

"Boring."

"The case?"

"The person."

"Do you know her well?"

"Better than I want to. She drives men batty. She's great with her eyes and hands, but I'm not crazy about her mime act."

"Jealous?"

"There are people who will tell you that. Vincent and I had a thing going for a while. He did the same dance other men do over her, and I didn't like that."

"Were they lovers?"

"I don't think so. Vincent would have bragged. But she was his model and that was bad enough. I went to his studio a few times. It was like watching Salome do her dance. She was into power."

"Where's his studio?"

"He has one of those big lofts south of Market. Near China Basin, across from the San Francisco RV Park. It's an alleyway on Lusk and Townsend. Vincent's making that area the place to be for artists."

"But now he's a director."

"New obsession. He's still at his studio at first light."

Goldilocks looked at her watch and then swallowed her drink. "Cuckoo clock says I gotta run."

I followed her over to the theatre and saw her to one of

the side doors. "Thank you," I said, "and one last question, not related to the case. A boring question for you, I'm sure . . ."

She interrupted. "How'd I get the name Goldilocks?"

"Right."

"Maybe you're not such a good detective. Maybe you should figure it out. Maybe I should put you on the case. Maybe I should have you nose around."

There was one answer. "Maybe."

"My publicist would tell you it's because my first performance was in second grade where I starred in *Goldilocks and the Three Bears*. But he's a fag and a liar."

"And what would you tell me?"

"Oh, I've got lots of stories. Some of them I almost believe. But a detective likes truth, doesn't he?"

I nodded.

She turned her back on me, then suddenly whirled about and raised her long flower skirt. She wasn't wearing underwear. Her pubic area was gold.

"Not your usual peroxide blonde, huh?"

She lowered her dress, slowly, and held my eyes. "I give performances people don't forget," she said, and then Goldilocks was gone.

I stared at the closed door and finally spoke. " 'Someone's been playing with my head,' growled Papa Bear."

8

I REMEMBERED TO RING Ellen's doorbell only once. The observant investigator even noticed the little sign this time, the one that read, I CAN'T HEAR KNOCK. PLEASE USE BELL. I wasn't very late, not even sociably late. Ellen greeted me with a big smile and ushered me in. I noticed all of her handiwork was put away this time, perhaps to tell me this night was for more than business. An iced bucket of white wine sitting prominently in the living room told me a little more.

"I think the wine needs to age another fifteen minutes," I said. "I don't want my fingers to slur, and Will Harrady is on Eastern time."

"And what time are you on?"

"Borrowed."

Ellen's TDD was in her study. I listened to her instructions. The GA button meant "go ahead," and when you finished with your transmission you hit SK twice. Ellen dialed Harrady's number. There was some flashing of lights on the TDD. I readied my fingers at the keyboard while a response came on the screen.

HELLO.

I began my typing.

Hello, Mr. Harrady. My name is Stuart Winter. I

71

am a private investigator calling from San Francisco.
I was wondering whether you would answer some
questions for me.

QUESTIONS REGARDING WHAT?

Questions regarding the disappearance of Anita
Walters. Did you know that she's missing?

NO, I DIDN'T.

You wouldn't have any idea where she is then?

NO, I WOULDN'T.

Has Anita tried to contact you since she left
Greenmont?

NO.

And you haven't been back in the area since you
left?

NO.

Why did you leave?

PERSONAL REASONS.

Personal reasons involving Anita Walters?

I DON'T LIKE YOUR WORD "INVOLVING." IT
HAS A PEJORATIVE CONNOTATION. IT PRE-
SUMES GUILT. I AM NOT GUILTY.

What are you not guilty of?

LIVING OUT NABOKOV'S FANTASIES.

You weren't involved with Anita?

I WAS INVOLVED WITH STUPIDITY.

Were you involved with Mrs. Lockhart?

The word was slow in appearing.

YES.

Tell me about your stupidity.

I BECAME PERSONAL WITH ANITA, BUT
NOT INVOLVED. I LISTENED TO HER PROB-
LEMS. I EVEN TOOK HER TO COFFEE A FEW
TIMES. THAT WAS NAIVE TO SAY THE LEAST.

Tell me about her problems.
I'M INCLINED TO SAY THOSE SHOULD RE-
MAIN CONFIDENTIAL.

I was getting tired of that sticky wicket.

And I'm inclined to argue. She might be in danger.
She might need help. There are some very worried
people. I need your knowledge.

Nothing appeared on the screen for a long time. Will
Harrady weighed my words and his thoughts. The steam
finally worked on the clam.

I DON'T THINK I CAN HELP YOU WITH ANY
REVELATIONS. ANITA HAD THE INSECURI-
TIES AND USUAL PROBLEMS OF EVERY
YOUNG WOMAN—WELL, SHE HAD MORE AN-
GER THAN USUAL. WHAT YOU SAW AND
WHAT WAS THERE TURNED OUT TO BE TWO
DIFFERENT THINGS.
Meaning?
EVEN BEHIND HER SMILE THERE WAS AN-
GER.
Who or what was she angry at?
WE REALLY DIDN'T GET TO SPECIFICS.
How about some nonspecifics?
SHE SAID SHE HATED INSENSITIVE PEOPLE.
I THINK HER PARENTS MADE THAT LIST. SHE
ONCE TOLD ME SHE HATED HER FATHER.
Anything else? Anyone else?
NO. OR YES. EVERYONE AND NO ONE.
Why were you dismissed from Greenmont?

I waited on his words again. He finally responded.

BECAUSE I WASN'T INNOCENT ENOUGH. AND NEITHER WAS ANITA.

What do you mean?

SHE HAD A CRUSH ON ME. I THINK I WAS HER FIRST LOVE. I DIDN'T LEAD HER ON. IT'S THE KIND OF THING THAT HAPPENS TO TEACHERS. YOU GET USED TO IT AND USUALLY IT'S KIND OF LOVELY AND KIND OF COMIC. BUT MORE LOVELY. AND I GUESS I WAS FLATTERED THAT SUCH A PRETTY YOUNG LADY FELT THAT WAY.

How flattered?

NOT *LOLITA* FLATTERED.

In what way wasn't she innocent enough?

SHE DIDN'T KNOW ABOUT LOVE. BUT SHE KNEW ABOUT HATE. IT WAS LIKE SHE HAD EATEN THE APPLE BEFORE BEING SHOWN TO THE GARDEN. KNOWLEDGE AND HATE BEFORE LOVE. NOT THE USUAL ORDER.

And in what way weren't you innocent enough?

I EXPECTED THE LOVE. MAYBE I NURTURED IT. BUT I DIDN'T IMAGINE HER HATE.

Tell me about both.

WE WERE WALKING ONE DAY. WE WERE AWAY FROM THE SCHOOL. AND SHE STARTLED ME BY PUTTING HER ARM AROUND ME, NOT LIKE FRIENDS, BUT LOVERS. I TRIED TO JOKE ABOUT THE WAY SHE WAS HOLDING ME, TRIED TO BE GENTLE, AND DISENTANGLE MYSELF. BUT THEN SHE STARTED KISSING ME, DESPERATELY KISSING ME, AND THAT SCARED ME. SHE WOULDN'T LET GO, WOULDN'T LISTEN TO ME, JUST KEPT KISSING ME AND SIGNING HOW MUCH SHE LOVED ME. SO I GRABBED HER ARMS AND SHOOK THEM AND HER UNTIL SHE FELL

LOOSE FROM ME, AND THEN I PUSHED HER
AWAY. I WAS SHAKEN, BUT NOT LIKE ANITA.
JUDAS DIDN'T DESERVE SUCH A LOOK OF
REPROACHMENT. I TRIED TO TALK TO HER
ABOUT LOVE, TRIED TO EXPLAIN, FINALLY
EVEN TRIED TO REACH AND COMFORT HER,
BUT WHEN I DID THAT SHE RAN AWAY.

How did you lose your job?

IT WAS THE NEXT DAY. ANITA CAME TO
MY SECOND-PERIOD CLASS BUT SHE DIDN'T
LINGER AFTER THE BELL LIKE USUAL. I
THOUGHT I'D GIVE HER HURT TIME,
THOUGHT I'D WAIT A FEW DAYS AND TALK
WITH HER IN PRIVATE. AFTER THIRD PERIOD
I ALWAYS HAVE A BREAK. I WAS GRADING
PAPERS IN MY CLASSROOM WHEN I SAW THE
DOOR OPEN. IT WAS ANITA. I GREETED HER,
BUT SHE DIDN'T SIGN BACK. SHE WALKED
SLOWLY TO THE FRONT OF THE ROOM, AND
STARTED UNBUTTONING HER BLOUSE. I
SIGNED FOR HER TO STOP, BUT SHE
WOULDN'T. I STARTED WALKING AWAY.
THAT'S WHEN SHE GRABBED MY NECK AND
HELD ON. AND THAT'S WHEN DEIDRE—MRS.
LOCKHART—WALKED IN.

Who factually reported she caught you entwined
with a half-naked student?

RIGHT. I THINK SHE BELIEVED ME WHEN I
EXPLAINED. I THINK THE BOARD BELIEVED
ME TOO. BUT JUST GOING OUT WITH STU-
DENTS IS VERBOTEN, EVEN IF THAT'S AL-
WAYS BEEN AN OVERLOOKED RULE. SO I
SUPPLIED MY OWN ROPE. BUT THEY DID LET
ME RESIGN.

What was Anita's story?

SHE REFUSED TO COMMENT. BUT MRS.

LOCKHART DID SAY SHE BELIEVED ANITA SAW HER WALKING TOWARD MY CLASS-ROOM.

What about you and Mrs. Lockhart?

UNDER THE CIRCUMSTANCES, SHE DIDN'T THINK SHE COULD BE SEEN WITH ME.

Do you hate Anita for what she did?

NOT ANYMORE. FOR A WHILE I TRIED TO FIGURE OUT WHAT COULD HAVE DRIVEN HER TO DO SUCH A THING. HELL HATH NO FURY NOTWITHSTANDING, THAT DIDN'T SEEM REASON ENOUGH. IF YOU EVER FIND OUT, TELL ME.

I will. Thank you for all your consideration.

HOW LONG HAS SHE BEEN MISSING?

Six months.

GOOD LUCK IN YOUR HUNT.

I thanked him once more and told him to call or teletype my office if he thought of anything else that might help my search. I took the printout of our conversation and tried to look at it for a minute, but my eyes and head rebelled at about the same time. I didn't object when Ellen led me to the living room. She had been by my side during the call, and we knew better than to talk about it or much of anything. She handed me a glass of wine and sat down next to me as she had at our first meeting, but this time there weren't chairs separating us. The wine was cold, and she was warm, and in the laws of nature and man that makes mush. There was a dinner behind the drink, one that a lot of planning had gone into, a roast with all the fixings. I objected all the way to the first bite.

I felt comfortable and relaxed, and the after dinner drinks smoothed away the last rough edges of a rough day. Our conversation had consisted mostly of my compliments and Ellen's responses to them. Now there wasn't the dinner between us, and we were at the time where friends wouldn't have lingered quite so long, and lovers would already have begun their love. It's the uncomfortable time when you feel you have to truck your words along your tongue, and dump them over the edge, and then feel a little stupid, and a little excited, because you can be stupid and still be forgiven, encouraged even, by smiles and looks.

But there was still that logical voice that asked questions without easy answers. She sensed some of the stop signs in my head. "What are you thinking?"

"That I have to be up before sunrise."

"Yes," she said, agreeing, and then nestled her body close to mine and started stroking my chest.

I looked at her, and thought of another name besides Ellen. Lolita. And then I tried to deny that other name, tried to tell myself that thirty-six was still young, still vital enough to be with her. I ran my hand through her hair, and it brushed against her ear and her hearing aid. I didn't pull away, but instead followed the contours of her lobe. Her hair covered some scar tissue around her ear, the stigmata of what I guessed was an operation. I thought to ask her about it, but asked something else I believed more important, even if I kept telling myself it wasn't.

"How old are you?"

"Twenty-one. Last week."

"So you were in high school until you were twenty?"

"In California the disabled can stay in high school through their twenty-first year. But for my last two years at Greenmont I wasn't technically in high school. I was an aide, which allowed me to get paid and get college credit."

"But you roomed with a student?"

"There's a housing shortage. I didn't see the need to demand my own room. And since Anita roomed with me when I was a senior and she was a sophomore, we just continued on that way."

"For three years?"

"Yes."

"Is it uncommon to have older deaf students in high school?"

"Not too. We have more to learn, remember?"

She kissed me, and contradicted her last statement. I tried to say something, make some feeble protest.

"I can't hear you," she said firmly.

"Good," I said.

The words fell on deaf ears, and so eventually did I.

I wasn't ready for a morning after, and was glad Ellen slept while I gathered my clothes. At first I crept around in the half darkness, and tried to not even breathe loudly, but then I remembered. I didn't whistle, but dressed easier not having to worry about making noise. I left a note in the kitchen, and then walked out to the Olds.

I would have liked a shower, a long, hot shower with plenty of soap, and a shave. I felt dirty, not only because my clothes were soiled and my breath could be distilled, but because I had violated one of my rules. As an investigator it's important to observe. That's the job, and you don't get involved, because that can interfere with the work. Involvement means sometimes you don't think right, and don't act right, and subsequently don't clean right.

Like last night.

And maybe this morning.

I didn't feel all repentant. Part of me felt very good. Part of me wanted to dwell on the stirrings going on inside. Part of me wanted to drive back to Oakland, and make a breakfast, and linger over coffee and talk. But I didn't stop. I followed the just-rising sun over the Bay Bridge, and drove to China Basin.

I parked on Townsend across from the RV park in front of Maxilla & Mandible. The name stood for truth in advertising. It was a bone store, featuring skeletal remains of animals. And humans. It must have been a morbid impulse that prompted me to put my hands to the window and look inside. Rows of bones lined the walls and displays, remains of the hoofed and the horned, the quick and the very dead. It was a good thing the store wasn't yet open, for I had an irresistible impulse to walk in and yell, "The name's Samson, and I'd like a jawbone of an ass."

But the doors were closed, so I sought other ways of making an ass of myself.

Goldilocks's directions were less than inspired. I wandered around Townsend and Lusk and settled on what must have been the right alley. The area was undergoing renovation, the old brick structures being set aright again. A lot of old warehouse buildings were still standing, and more than a few were being refurbished. Layers of whitewash had been applied to the brick buildings, but you could still read some of the old names, like Cleveland Van and Storage, and Ogden Packing. In back of the alley were railroad tracks long in disuse, and home now only for a lot of shattered glass.

I walked up the alley back to Townsend and stood looking around. The China Basin Building had undergone a nice facelift, and showed its six floors of red and black proudly. I heard a door close, and turned to the sound.

A man was muttering into his goatee. He looked like he was in active search of his muse or his mind. I stepped into his path and got his attention.

"Where's Vincent's studio?"

He took one hand out of his pocket, pointed to the loft across the street, then walked by and continued on with his conversation. It was a three-story building, one of half a dozen converted loft structures in the alley. There wasn't a doorbell. I tried the doorknob and it turned.

There were hard wood floors leading in several directions. They had the wear of years on them, and probably hadn't been waxed since their installation. The place was old and drafty. The once white interior paint was gray and chipped, which didn't explain the strong smell of paint in the air, so I followed my nose. If, as some insist, I'm a son of a bitch, then I claim my heritage as bloodhound. My nose led me up complaining stairs, paused to sniff for a few moments on the second floor, then directed me up one more flight. I wandered a hall and settled in front of some large sliding fire doors. They had probably been installed to comply with a housing regulation decades past. I used the metal grips to separate the doors, and slid them on worn tracks to the right and left. The exposed area looked big enough to house a basketball court, but it was an art studio, a messy and occupied art studio.

Two sets of eyes looked at me. Vincent's comprised one pair, a naked woman's the other. She was cold. She was also weirdly positioned on her back, her arms and legs in the air.

"You are the private detective."

Vincent had an impressive bass. He was well posed in front of his easel, brush in hand. I dislike artifice, and despise others who make me part of their set. I got the feeling that Vincent would have preferred me positioned like the model, or maybe a pinned butterfly. I started walking and looking around the studio, the very dirty studio, while I talked.

"I am. My name is Stuart Winter."

"And you wish to know about Anita Walters?"

"Yes."

"Vincent will answer a few questions, but this is his time to create. When Vincent tells you to leave, you will leave."

"Fair enough."

"Your first question is, 'Do you know where Anita is?' Vincent does not."

"When did you last see her, Mr . . . ?"

"I am Vincent."

"I'm not comfortable with first names. Your last name is?"

"My entire name is Vincent. You may call me Mr. Vincent if that pleases you."

It didn't. I kicked some cigarette butts, and papers, and the solitary name, out of my path. I didn't kick gently. There was a pattern of colors revealed under my feet, but it was hard to tell whether they had been painted, or were residue. Tubes of paint were strewn everywhere, and between slashed paintings and broken pallets you could see how colors had run into the concrete. There was enough junk food thrown around to keep both the cockroaches and the memory of Dan White's Twinkie defense alive. There were nails, and canvas strips, and discarded sketches. The naked models must have loved walking around there.

"So when did you last see her, Vince?"

He pretended not to notice the abbreviation. "December thirty-first."

"And how do you remember that date?"

"We wished each other a Happy New Year."

"She said that to you?"

"No. Vincent said it to her. And she motioned the same from her to me."

I didn't know whether it was proper etiquette for a bystander to notice a naked model, but she was almost blue and our hot air wasn't helping her. July was only a few days away, but her goose bumps didn't know that. The building was cold.

"Maybe she can take five?" I asked, and got a grateful smile for my request.

"We won't be that long."

I looked at Vincent. He was about my age, not quite as tall as I am, but a bit broader. I doubted whether paintbrushes alone had produced his muscles. His beard was thick and black, and like Mrs. Houston had said, it made his face difficult to read. There was a lot of energy in the

man. His hands were active, something he didn't consciously control. Every minute or so his right index finger
jabbed out, then pushed forward under his left palm. It
was almost as if he were washing his hands with a twist.
It was hard to concentrate on his words when confronted
by his tic. He and Captain Queeg probably would have
gotten along just fine.

"How did you meet Anita?"

"Through another artist friend. She modeled for several
of us."

"How long did she model for you?"

"A few months."

"Every day?"

"Most days."

"You paid her?"

"Very well."

"You had performances put on in her apartment. Why?"

"She volunteered her apartment."

"But the performances were directed at her. Why would
a model get so much special attention?"

He spoke through his tic. "Vincent needed Anita for
evaluation purposes, someone without ears. *Secret Societies* will appeal to all senses. It won't need music. It won't
need words. It will project itself on many levels."

"*Secret Societies* is the name of your play?"

"Yes."

"Did you choose the Masonic Temple for its premier?"

"What could be more appropriate? And ironic?"

"Where is the irony?"

"The Masons are called a secret society, but they are really the opposite. They are old, dying men with hand-
shakes, rings, and some comic mumbo jumbo. The real
secret societies are found in individuals. They are in the
thoughts of each of us. And sometimes actions."

"How were you able to gauge Anita's reactions to the
performances?"

His moving hand went from a slashing turn to a simpatico patting motion of his head, something he didn't even notice. "We were attuned. Se didn't need words. Vincent read her. She communicated what was missing."

"So the deaf will appreciate your play?"

"Yes. But it's not designed for just the deaf, just the living. Vincent wanted to analyze the roots of performance, of art, to learn and relearn the many ways it appeals, and how it can appeal. Vincent didn't want to be dependent on just sight, or sound, or smell. You can touch in many ways, and we will."

"So Anita was a guinea pig?"

"One of many. Vincent has brought together many perspectives, many viewpoints. A blind man also reviewed the performances."

"And they were performed at his place?"

"Yes."

I stepped close to the model. Her legs were in the air, somewhat reminiscent of a dog in wait of a stomach scratching. I refrained.

"What kind of model is Anita?"

"A good one. She needed to be retrained from her photography days. She needed to learn patience. But she was never easily distracted."

"I understand you were attracted to her."

Gods are not supposed to fall for mortals. It goes against the rules. Vincent reminded me.

"If anything, it was the reverse. Vincent is not without his admirers. Looks are not enough to attract Vincent."

"But she fell for you?"

"She came here when Vincent needed. She took her clothes off when Vincent told her. She posed in whatever way Vincent said."

"You make her sound like your slave."

"Vincent is a slave to art. It commands him. Vincent submits to it. It is the one that orders, not Vincent."

I sauntered over to Vincent's painting. I didn't think much of his latest orders. The painting depicted a birth. A woman, a model, as being born. She, a woman of about twenty-five, was coming out of a baby. She looked confused, and bloody, and angry. The baby birthing her looked serene.

"Do you like it?"

"No."

Vincent looked pleased. "Why not?"

"I like Constable and Turner. I like clear images. I distrust disorder and conflicting messages. Your work isn't clean enough for me."

Sometimes the elephant does notice the flea. "Unless snooping pays very, very well, you could never afford the price anyway."

"Unless I'm a very, very good snoop."

"If you were, you wouldn't be here." I think Vincent smiled behind his beard.

"Are you shown in a particular gallery?"

"No. But Vincent is having a special exhibition tomorrow."

"Where?"

He tried, but not very hard, to keep the braggadocio out of his voice. "The San Francisco Museum of Modern Art."

"Will you be giving a talk?"

"Yes."

"Maybe you'll spare me a minute there." I gathered myself to leave, but then acted like I remembered something. I pointed to a large shed in the corner. It was well fortified, with formidable-looking locks. "What's that for?"

"My works, even unfinished works, are very valuable. This is a less than secure building. I sometimes store them in there."

"May I see?"

I was clearly pushing the moment, but Vincent yielded

with a sigh. He walked over to the armored shed. I took a moment to follow, and paused to slip my card and a twenty into the model's hand. She palmed them, not having much else of a choice in the way of a hiding place.

Vincent found the appropriate key and opened the door. There was a lot of unused space inside. A few canvases lay on their sides. It smelled of turpentine. Compared to the loft, it was surprisingly clean. Vincent looked at me for comment, but I didn't have one. I knocked on the shed's wall. It was thick enough to almost completely retard the sounds.

"You will have to leave now," he said impatiently. "Vincent has much work to do."

"Okay."

I was slow in shuffling out. He was already at work when I walked by the canvas again. "What will you call it?"

"Birthing Pains."

I kept walking, turning back at the door only when Vincent started mumbling. But he wasn't talking to me. He was talking at his painting. Something there bothered him. His tic took on a violent quality, and then he threw down his brush. He grabbed some tubes of paint. Groaning, snorting, he pulled off their caps and then turned the tubes on his model. He squirted the paint at her, squeezed it out with his big hands. The paint arced and streamed. He went through four or five tubes, dropping one empty after another on the floor until crisscrossing trails of red ran the length of the model's body. She looked too frightened to move. Her mouth was open, and some spittle ran down her chin, spittle that mixed with the red paint. Vincent's noises stopped, replaced instead by the enthusiastic sounds of his slapping the paint around the model. His hands pressed the paint on her white flesh, rubbing it around her stomach and breasts and pubic area and legs. He did it none too gently.

"That's it," he said, "that's it."

I don't think he noticed me watching the door, and I didn't stay around to see if he'd use the tears dropping from the model's eyes in his painting. I was only grateful he wasn't telling his model to make love to the canvas.

9

A CLEAN SHIRT, A razor, and mouthwash awaited me at my office, and sometimes that's about as much as you can ask out of life. The lavatory down the hall was unoccupied, so I gave myself a sink bath. After cleaning, I drank a cup of coffee and tried to stir some gray cells. Rodin wouldn't have unpacked his chisel for me. I shifted some papers around on my desk and accomplished nothing, so I dialed Miss Tuntland for inspiration.

"Hello."

"Morning."

"Do you look like you sound?" Her inquiry bordered between solicitous and mocking

"I take it that's not a compliment."

"You are a detective, aren't you?"

"Just another investigator looking for Rosebud."

"Looking very late. I called you last night." Her voice was neutral.

"And I can guess what you called me." My accent wasn't bad, but it needed the cigar and beetle brows as props. Miss Tuntland didn't laugh, so I quite properly assumed she had never heard of Groucho.

"I worked late," I said, "and was working again at dawn."

"And was it worth it?"

And were word games? "We'll see. Last night I talked with a deaf man who lived across the country."

"He must have had some hearing aid."

Her Groucho was better than mine, but my ego prevented me from laughing. "And early this morning I met with an artist. Or artisté. He calls himself Vincent. I don't think I'd like to see his self-portrait."

Miss Tuntland let me ramble a little more, heard enough of my complaints, and a few of my whines, then interrupted. "Are you calling to ask for some help?"

I didn't need to think about it. "Yes."

"Let me put you on hold. I have another call."

She wasn't long, and didn't need to be reminded where we left off. "Okay. Now what am I supposed to do?"

"I'd like Vincent's real name. He's having an exhibition tomorrow at the Museum of Modern Art. They might be able to supply that information. Or call a few galleries. I'd be interested in any gossip. You should also expect a call from a woman who's going to be very tentative. She's Vincent's model. I slipped her a bill and my card."

"Why don't you like Vincent?"

"He's dirty," I said, "and he's a fanatic. Thinks his visions are inspired. Probably needs four seats to sit down. One for him, and three more for the supporting cast of the Trinity behind him."

Miss Tuntland didn't seem as inclined to my prejudice. "A lot of artists are affected," she said. "Society gives them that dispensation, even if private detectives don't. And the ego's necessary. It's protective. Even the best artists have had to live with terrible rejection. Van Gogh only sold one painting in his lifetime."

She sounded like she knew what she was talking about. Her "Gogh" rhymed with "awk." Dutch pronunciations and bird cries always pique my interest.

"Sounds like this is personal to you," I said.

"I paint," she said.

Behind those two words were a lot of pictures hidden in closets. "And I'll bet you paint very well," I said. "But even if you become a successful artist you won't start using your own name in a sentence, and that's what Vincent does. How would you like it if I said, "Winter is going to be out today?" Or, "Winter doesn't operate that way?"

"I suppose that depends on how Winter does operate."

We were playing the old movies today; first my Groucho, then hers, and now her Mae West. I further unfocused the projector, put a little James Cagney and grapefruit grinding in the scene. "Winter would like to operate right now by tweaking Tuntland's nose. And Winter thanks Tuntland for her concern. And for her extra work."

The good thing about rental cars is that they are test models. The winding Berkeley Hills are perfect for rentals, almost as good as some of the back roads in Napa Valley. The Olds was put through all of the tests. While a little sluggish on acceleration, it performed admirably in handling and braking. I was almost by 1211 Overhill Drive when I noticed the hanging-by-a-rusty-thread sign that announced my location. I used the two-foot brake method on a curve going around fifty. The car fishtailed a little, but not much. The test drive ended off the main road and inches from a gate.

I got out of the Olds and opened the gate. A gravel driveway losing a battle to wild grass, and encroached on both sides by brush, was civilization's only path. I drove a little ways forward, followed the posted instructions to the rusty letter by getting out and closing the gate, then slowly crunched the car along a mostly upward ascent for almost a third of a mile. The gravel ended at a sprawling, shabby, ranch house. To the side of the house were two bungalow-type structures. Bridging the bungalows was a fully enclosed link fence that opened up to a grass enclosure complete with jungle gyms.

Half a dozen other cars were parked in the driveway, but no one was in sight. The place was more quiet and private than the one-ring circus I expected. There was no road noise, and the grounds were silent. A horror writer would have called them ominously silent. I looked around, and waited for something to happen. When nothing did, I grew bothered. Something far older than memory signaled. It was hot enough outside for a hot sweat, but mine was cold. The hairs on my neck prickled. Behind the house a dog started to bark. A faint scratching started, then stopped, then started again. I followed the sound to its source.

I half laughed. It reminded me of the primatologist who locked one of his experimental chimps in a bedroom. He said he wanted a keyhole view of how the chimp would react to his new environment. But when he bent down and peered through the keyhole, all he saw was a very brown eye peering back.

Primates are the most popular attraction at every zoo in the world. Nonhuman primates I should say. Between gorillas and homo sapiens there is less than a two-percent difference in genetic makeup. One of my kissing cousins stared at me from a small, wired window in the bungalow nearest to me. I felt better for his presence, even believed he had scratched the window just to reassure me.

His head started moving back and forth in a rolling motion. Since neither one of us was at sea, and the window was at about the six-foot level, I guessed he was propped up by a tire.

Our eye contact was interrupted when the door to the bungalow opened, and an intense young man walked out. "Please go inside the house," he said quietly but firmly, "or else I'll never get Joseph's attention. We have his lessons to attend to."

A raspberry reverberated from the window. It was a good raspberry, had a lot of lip and Bronx in it, and a lot of recalcitrant schoolboy. It brought my first smile of the day.

"That's Joseph?" I asked.

The man nodded.

I pointed at the house. "Will I find Dr. Harrison in there?"

"Yes. Don't bother ringing the doorbell. It doesn't work. Just walk in."

I took his advice and was at the door when Joseph unleashed a second raspberry. I realized my rudeness, and stopped to wave at him. He didn't wave back, didn't perform, just continued to stare. I reluctantly stopped waving, wiped my neck with a handkerchief, then pushed the door open and called out a greeting.

No one called back, and as self-guided tours are usually the most interesting, I set out on one. There must have once been a living room in the ranch house, but the area had long since been usurped by piles of books and periodicals and gorilla memorabilia. The room was decorated in a gorilla motif. There were wind-up apes, stuffed gorillas, china gorillas, and all manner of trinket gorillas. Gorilla visages abounded, from benign to terrifying. The walls were lined with pictures and paintings and framed photographs. The Gorilla Project had its share of celebrity followers. Some well-known figures, actors, and politicians were posed in pictures with the gorillas and what I assumed was Dr. Harrison. The gorillas and the doctor didn't smile for the photos, but their guests had plenty to spare.

I lingered over a huge box of photos that would never find an album. I hoped to find a picture of Anita at work, but humans were definitely second banana to the apes. When I finished with the photos I moved on to a stuffed gorilla in the corner. There was a lot of dust on him and his cymbals. I wiped him, and wound him, and he played with considerable clatter.

"What do you want?"

The voice belonged to a face made familiar by the photographs. Dr. Harrison was about fifty, tall and thin. He was spectacled, and even behind his glasses you could see the dark circles under his eyes. His hair was mostly silver and three weeks too long. Harrison's height was negated by his stoop. His shoulders were permanently bent forward, the position of yet another one of Atlas's successors. He wasn't an unhandsome man, but he had been tired for too long. Harrison was undoubtedly the chief, and by the looks of it, indifferent and overworked, administrator. If he had been more of a diplomat he would have been driving on a paved driveway, and probably had a sinecure at some university. He didn't look like he knew how to compromise, and the prospect of his learning was dim. He was too harried to remember social graces, either that or he didn't give a damn about them. The toy gorilla stopped clanging and I spoke.

"My name's Stuart Winter. I had an appointment to see you. I'm a private investigator looking into the disappearance of Anita Walters."

Harrison bit his lip, and the word "damn," at the same time. "I forgot." It was an explanation, not an apology. "And today is not a good day."

"I won't take up too much time."

He opened his pursed lips, and threw me a verbal penny. "Very well. You may follow me around and ask your questions while I work, provided you do not interfere." I followed him. The living room looked organized compared to what must have been the main office. Two volunteers opened envelopes in one room and answered phones. A large pile of letters waited hopefully next to a word processor. A bulletin board was littered with reminders, and an oversized calendar was blackened with entries. I could feel the fat finger of the little Dutch boy all around.

We were joined in the room by a woman who carried her world on a clipboard. I wasn't introduced, but it was clear that she, and her clipboard, were the only things between civilization and the Visigoths. Point one was a reminder to Harrison about the news team coming at three. Point two was that someone had to go into town for the food pickup because Ted wasn't coming today. And point three wasn't entirely a point but a question: since Barbara wasn't coming in until two for Ted's shift, who was going to take Joseph between noon and two?

The phones started ringing, and over them Harrison announced he'd handle both the grocery pickup and the teaching chores. The Point Woman's clipboard was hardly empty, but Harrison didn't wait to hear more. He walked out the back door, and I followed. Two large oak trees and a lot of manzanita took up the distant expanse, but close to the house the land had been cleared and tilled. A flat tract stretched for about fifty square yards. Shoots were springing up, some several feet tall. Harrison paused to examine one, then remembered me.

"Bamboo," he said. "The gorillas love it."

We walked around to the driveway and got in an old pickup. It started on the third try. I appreciated my rental's suspension that much more as we barreled along. Harrison drove quickly. His inclination was toward silence, but I took advantage of the relative peace and talked over the noise of the engine.

"Tell me about Anita."

"A good worker."

"Which means?"

"Always on time. Willing to work extra. Not continually going out of town."

"Are most of your staff volunteers?"

"Yes."

"I take it money's tight?"

"I haven't drawn a salary in the last five years."

"How do you get funding?"

"We have our membership. And there's always our begging."

Harrison would starve, I was sure, before his gorillas.

"Is it hard getting teachers?"

"Yes. You have to either be, or become familiar with, Ameslan—American Sign Language. And then you have to sit with the gorillas for hours on end and encourage them to participate. That's the hard part. They could learn quickly enough if they wanted to, but they're smart enough to want to do other things. There's a lot of repetition that makes for some boring sessions."

The boredom he mentioned was in his voice. It was clear his interest wasn't in humans, missing or not. He lived and breathed his gorillas twenty-four hours a day. There was no other world for him. I put Anita in the proper context.

"How many gorillas do you have here?"

"Two. Anita's charge was Joseph."

"Why that name?"

"Biblical. Remember Joseph and his coat of many colors? Our Joseph is a lowland gorilla, a silverback. His coat's mostly black, but as he matures it will become more silver. In the right light you can see red, too."

"What's the other gorilla's name?"

"Bathsheba. We've had them since they were babies. Their mothers were killed by poachers. Gorilla-paw ashtrays are considered very chic in some parts of the world."

There wasn't outrage in his voice, there was reasoned death. Not the reasoned death of the gorillas, but of the poachers, and those who would drop their ashes in such a hand. Having pronounced death, Harrison remembered himself.

"The names were provided by missionaries. They were brought to the mission as babies, and cared for by them."

"Tell me about the project."

"It's a lifelong project. The gorillas are very special. They have vocabularies upwards of six hundred words. They sign in response to questions, or independently initiate conversation. We have tapes of them talking—signing—to themselves."

"I've heard they lie."

"I prefer the word 'equivocate.' They're like children. If they've done something naughty, they'll blame the other for what they've really done. Or if you ask them to show you a color, and they feel contrary, they'll purposely display every other color than the one you asked for."

"What were Anita's responsibilities?"

"Basically everything. Like all teachers."

"Be specific."

"There's a lot to being a teacher. They have to instruct, and they have to observe. Most days the teachers are given a vocabulary list and told to test the gorillas on those words, make them sign or show they understand them. And there are other daily worksheets teachers have to keep current. They have to note whether the gorillas spontaneously sign, or if they sign in relation to stimuli, and how they sign, under what conditions, et ceterea, et cetera. The teachers also have to take care of feeding the gorillas, and keep track of their diet."

"How long are the shifts?"

"Four to five hours."

"Are they very structured?"

"Yes and no. There's always work to do, but the teachers know the gorillas are more responsive if they have some diversions from their lessons. Some teachers read to them, or play music. They prefer classical, you know."

His last remark seemed fatuous, and set me off. "No, I didn't. But, I'm willing to bet Anita didn't discuss Bach with Joseph, and didn't read to him either, since she's both deaf and nonverbal."

Harrison gave me a quick glance, then calmly responded. "There are many ways to interact with the gorillas. There is a bonding between teacher and gorilla. They find matters of mutual interest. I know Joseph and Anita used to play 'chase' quite a bit."

He made the sign with his hands, two fists coming together horizontally.

"And I know she brought in magazines and picture books and turned the pages for him to see."

"You witnessed her teaching?"

"Of course. And I always read her logs."

"Logs?"

"All teachers keep a log of every session. They record basically everything that goes on in their shift. Why did Joseph go and look out his window? Was there noise? And how did he react to visitors? Anything at all."

"May I see those logs?"

"Later, yes."

We pulled into the parking lot of a supermarket and drove around to the back. I followed Harrison through a door marked EMPLOYEES ONLY. He greeted a few box boys and a butcher, and then found the manager. Everyone appeared slightly amused by Harrison, this scarecrow figure who moved so quickly, but I noticed their languid pace accelerated in his presence. Harrison briskly led the manager and me to the loading and unloading area. Maybe the man was a miracle worker. The manager pulled out a set of keys as if a stopwatch were on him, produced the right one, then turned it to open the metal delivery doors. Over their clatter he pointed out which crates were for the gorillas. Harrison knew the routine well enough to barely take notice. With one breath Harrison gave both perfunctory thanks and dismissal to the manager.

Some of the boxes and crates were heavy, and not a few were slimy. Harrison was quite content to have me take on the heavier loads. "Too bad the gorillas couldn't help with these," I said while tussling with one particularly bulky crate.

I saw Harrison smile a little, the proud father remembering. "They could carry them easily enough if they had a mind to, but I don't think we could get them to lift a finger. No, they'd be in the truck, probably honking with impatience."

"Do they ever ride in the truck?"

"Not anymore. They did when they were young. And if they'd been extra good during the day, I'd give them a soda for the ride. People always stared at us when we drove along the road. They'd look three or four times, even stop their cars. I was afraid we'd cause an accident."

"Are their riding days long past?"

"Twelve years past. People talk about kids growing up fast. They should see gorillas. Joseph's well over three hundred pounds now, and Bathsheba's over two hundred pounds."

I listened while struggling with another container. Harrison seemed to take some pleasure in my efforts. "You're a big man," he said. "How much do you weigh?"

"Two-twenty."

"And by human standards you're strong. But Joseph would have been able to beat you at arm wrestling by his first birthday. And now he's many, many, times stronger than you are."

"If his olfactory senses are many times stronger," I said, "I'm surprised he'd eat this food."

Harrison actually gave a little laugh, and told me it might be considered human bad, but it was certainly gorilla good. The Gorilla Project gratefully accepted the supermarket discards, the week-old lettuce, ten-day-old squash, the squishy tomatoes, growthy potatoes, bruised apples, misshapen oranges, and overripe eggplants. We finished filling the truck with fruits and vegetables and stale bread, and then started back. Harrison said the food would last for three or four days, which reminded me of an old gorilla joke. I wondered if Harrison had heard it.

"What do you give to a four-hundred-pound gorilla?" I asked.

"Anything he wants," said Harrison.

He was still able to smile at that one, so I knew it was safe to ask other questions.

"Do the gorilla workers do social things together?"

"Not too much. I try to throw an open dinner once a month. It's gorilla fare all the way. We're carrying a lot of good foods disguised as discards. Healthy soups, sauteed vegetables, eggplant parmesan, banana-nut bread, casseroles. You name it."

I did. "Indigestion." But I didn't say it out loud.

"How did Anita hear about the Gorilla Project?"

"I work with the administrators at Greenmont. They place some of their older students."

"Did you interview her?"

"Beyond saying, 'Thank you, Lord, for sending another body'? No. How many qualified people do you think are willing to donate their time? And how many will work for an old fussbudget like me who's usually too tired to give them a pat on the back and tell them what a fine and important job they're doing?"

"Was Anita friendly with anyone else at the project?"

"No. She pretty much arrived, worked with Joseph, then left. Sometimes she slept over in the guest house when the weather was bad. She didn't like the long drive back to the peninsula when it was wet."

"How many times did she sleep over?"

"I don't know. Maybe half a dozen times."

"Is that common for workers?"

"Not uncommon. We have several unused beds."

"Who else lives on the property as a rule?"

"We frequently have visitors, but I'm the only permanent inhabitant. That's probably why it's a mess."

"You're not married?"

"No," he said. We turned off the main road and drove

up to the gate. "But you may as well meet my family. Why don't you get out and open the gate?"

I met Bathsheba first. She had a woman teacher who didn't look pleased at our interruption. The teacher bore a resemblance to Bathsheba, but I liked the gorilla better. Bathsheba was more coquettish, and obviously cared more for men, and what she lacked in looks she made up in style. She draped herself in a blanket and sashayed as well as a gorilla can sashay round a cage. In an evening dress she might have passed muster. She blew me some kisses, but I have a firm rule against falling for someone hairier than myself.

Harrison asked some questions of the teacher while I watched Bathsheba. She had lots of toys and was interested in showing them to me. Her dowry, I supposed. She kept digging things out for display, but even when her back was turned she was attentive to everything going on in her house. The slightest movement brought a glance from her, as if she really did have eyes in the back of her head. A few times I guessed she was motioning to play, but I wasn't exactly sure what she wanted to do. She signed a few things at me, and I was frustrated because I couldn't respond.

"What's she saying?" I asked.

Harrison glanced over to interpret. In terms of signing, Bathsheba wasn't the best. Her hands weren't held up as high or as clearly as her human cousins, and her digits weren't as well formed. But she was saying something.

"Bathsheba love," translated Harrison.

Bathsheba took her hand and brought it under her teeth to make a little sound.

"And now she's signing for a nut. I'm afraid sometimes her love is inextricably combined with the wants of her stomach."

"May I give her a nut?"

"She's already been fed," the woman said.

"She doesn't exactly look like she's on a diet," I said.

Harrison became the diplomat. "I think it would be all right to give her a few nuts, don't you, Helen?"

Helen clearly didn't think so, but didn't say so to Harrison. She reluctantly gave me a handful of peanuts. I leaned forward, ready to put my hand through the bars.

"Do that, and chance losing a finger."

I was surprised Helen uttered a warning. I looked to Harrison for confirmation of danger.

"Bathsheba's playful," he admitted, "and she might decide to grab hold of your finger a little too hard and a little too long. I'm the only one who goes in the cage with her these days. But what you can do is let her reach out for the nuts, or you can put them on the floor."

I decided to be brave. No one's ever accused me of having small hands, but my fingers looked like toothpicks near Bathsheba's. Bathsheba took and then ingested the peanut. Then she reached for more. She was gentle about taking them, but expedient. She had my entire supply and was signing for more in less than a minute.

"That's enough, Bathsheba," said Harrison. Dad spoke, and Bathsheba stopped her begging. "Now what do you say?"

She flipped her wrists up, moved a couple of digits. "She said, 'Thank you.' "

"Why does her signing look so different from human signing?"

"We have flexible thumbs. And she's lazy. Ameslan has evolved, or devolved, to Gorillaslan. Sometimes you have to coax the gorillas to sign properly. They don't feel like making the effort to stretch their fingers, or linger on their words. Sometimes they slur."

Bathsheba was hanging from her legs on a suspended tire. With her head brushing the ground, and her body swinging back and forth, she signed at me.

"That's another problem with a gorilla signing," said

Harrison. "They do it anywhere, in any position. Most humans don't sign while hanging upside down."

"What's she saying?"

"She's asking for a drink."

"She has water."

"Bathsheba has a sweet tooth. She prefers fruit juice or soda."

At least she didn't prefer Scotch. I could see taking her to the Castle and calling out for drinks. But knowing the bartender, Mal, he probably wouldn't bat an eye. Polk Street was nearby.

Harrison had a few more things to discuss with Helen, so I continued to watch Bathsheba. She liked being the center of attention, liked my talking to her. I was surprised when she responded to my words. I told her to bring me a red rag, and she did. Flukes happen, so I asked if she wouldn't show me her robe. She took it off and waved it in front of my eyes. Then I asked her to go get her brush, and she went off to comply.

I turned to Harrison excitedly. I was surprised Bathsheba understood my commands so well, and wondered how many of my spoken words she had understood. But maybe what I should have wondered was how obedient she was to those same spoken words. Bathsheba was halfway to her brush when I turned my eyes from her. A human mind wouldn't have been able to react to a slight so quickly. Her two hundred pounds turned very quickly and very quietly, more quickly than two hundred pounds should ever turn. One second's inattention cost me a button.

"That's very bad, Bathsheba. Give the button back right now."

Harrison signed as he spoke. He was severe and Bathsheba looked chagrined. But she did bite the button first, learned it was an imitation pearl, then handed it back to Harrison. He dropped it in my hand with a "sorry."

"You were too close to the cage," said a sympathetic Helen.

"Maybe I like females to rip the buttons off my shirt," I said.

We left the room, the gorilla signing, "Bathsheba love, Bathsheba love," and the woman thinking, "Asshole, asshole." One admirer, one detractor. I beat my usual averages.

Outside I asked Harrison the question I had given up a button for: "How much of what we say do the gorillas understand?"

"Quite a bit. They know objects. They know the names of individuals. They can follow much of what you're saying as long as it relates to their world. E equals MC squared wouldn't mean much to them."

"Nor me. How smart are they?"

"IQ tests put them at eighty and up. Bathsheba and Joseph test close to a hundred."

"So why aren't they working for the government?"

We ended up at Joseph's bungalow. Harrison explained that he had to teach for the next two hours and preferred not to be interrupted. I bargained a little.

"I'd like to watch. Get an idea what Anita did. I won't be a bother."

He wavered, and I decided not to chance it. "And afterwards I'll store all the gorilla groceries."

That clinched it, and I followed Harrison inside. While Joseph was delighted to see papa, he was shy of me. For the first few minutes he appraised me from the corners of his eyes. Harrison told me not to take his actions personally, but to accept them as typical gorilla reactions to a stranger. That was before Joseph started bouncing against the walls. "Displaying," Harrison said. "Terrifying," I said. He was a San Francisco earthquake by himself. Gradually he quieted down. Between the banging, Harrison gave me a primer on gorilla etiquette.

You don't stare, especially at a male. That's a challenge. And you stay seated, and act submissive. There were a lot of other commandments and I tried to remember them. One was to speak in soothing, not loud, tones, and not to say or sign anything upsetting. I guess that included any hinting about his smell. Massive gorillas have an aroma all their own, and with the door closed I couldn't help but be ever more aware of that by the minute. It overwhelmed in close quarters, and promised to cling for some time to my hair and body.

Harrison and Joseph had a good rapport. They talked for a while, and every now and then Harrison translated. Joseph had seen a cat stalking a bird before, and Harrison asked him about that. From what Harrison could interpret, Joseph didn't think much of cats, but he did admire birds. Smart gorilla. Harrison asked Joseph whether he liked the way they flew, but Joseph stopped moving his digits. He went off in a corner and turned his back, not responding to Harrison's entreaty to come back.

"Sometimes he's like that," said Harrison. "Sometimes he doesn't want to be bothered. He thinks a lot, I know that. He broods, too. Gorillas don't truckle like chimpanzees. They don't please for pleasing. I'm convinced Joseph has deep thoughts. With his signing we get hints of that."

"Would he know Anita's name?"

"Yes. And her sign." Harrison made an A with his fingers. "But I'd prefer you wouldn't say her name to him."

"Why?"

"Gorillas form an attachment to their teachers. When Anita disappeared, he asked about her. They don't like it when their teachers leave. They don't like their environment changed."

There was a rapping at our door. It was the point lady and her clipboard. She hated to interrupt, but . . .

"I'll be back in a minute," said Harrison.

At Harrison's departure, Joseph slammed his arm

against the wall and then turned back to look at a reverberating me. I kept a firm grip on my seat. Joseph had several tires, one of which he propped against the wall. He balanced on that and looked out the window. Dr. Harrison and the point lady hadn't kept him interested for long. He approached the thick bars of the cage, then strummed them like a human would a harp. That rattled them and me.

I kept my eyes averted while looking at him, and he did the same with me. Then, surprisingly, he signed at me, and more surprisingly, I knew what he wanted. I got up, kept my back bent, and went over to the refrigerator. There were some nuts in there. I grabbed some and carefully proffered them to Joseph. He ate them and asked for more.

"Sorry, Joseph," I said. "All out."

I showed him my hands, and he seemed satisfied.

"What now?" I asked.

He signed again, and I was lucky. I knew "chase," too. Joseph shuffled along from side to side, and I followed his motions. We both enjoyed ourselves, though I made a point of not getting too near the bars. By mutual consent, five minutes of chase was enough. I sat down again, and both of us went back to surreptitiously observing the other. I suppose I shouldn't have, but it was a unique interview opportunity.

"Joseph," I said, "what happened to Anita?" I signed the name and repeated the question.

He stared at me, and I at him, for the first time. He seemed to consider the question in a calm, almost melancholy manner. Then he turned around and shuffled back to his window. He never looked back at me, even stopped acknowledging my presence with his side glances. He just looked out his window, out toward the back. He was the picture of someone in deep thought.

"If only he could talk," I thought, then remembered that he could. He just didn't want to.

10

I GAVE THE OLDS another workout in getting back to the City, and then parked illegally. My four o'clock appointment was pressing, but not as pressing as my need to wash. I smelled of gorillas and rotten vegetables and sweat. Ten minutes of lather and ten dollars of cologne made me smell like a dandy, but it beat the alternative.

My car hadn't been tagged by the police. I credited luck, or the threat from the opened windows. There was a definite lingering essence of Pongidae. My cologne fought back with mixed results. I left the windows open, but the Gorilla Project remained close to all of my senses during the drive to Bush Street. My nose directed my mind, and led it back to my last hour at the project.

When Harrison had returned to the bungalow, I excused myself for vegetable-moving duties. Afterward, I asked Harrison to let me look through the gorilla log book. He referred me to the point lady, who, with the imminent arrival of a news team, needed me like she did another entry on her crowded notepad. I coaxed her into letting me make copies of Anita's entries. The point lady really wasn't a bad sort; just another soul who had taken on a Sisyphean task. We talked over the hum of the copier. She was devoted to the project, devoted to Harrison, but there were "so many" problems. The plumbing didn't work sometimes; the gorillas were outgrowing their quarters; better heating was needed; why, even the bamboo had some kind of rot.

I asked her about the bamboo. Why had it been planted? And when?

"It's something we can't get through the supermarkets," she said, "and I'm told it's a special gorilla treat. Dr. Harrison planted it as his New Year's project."

"He planted in January?"

She nodded.

"Wasn't that an odd time to plant?"

"No odder than most of the things around here," she said.

The point lady noticed my missing button. I told her about Bathsheba's quick hands, and she told me I wasn't the first to suffer such a fate. I asked her whether the gorillas had ever hurt anyone unintentionally. She said she didn't think so, but that I should ask Dr. Harrison to be sure.

I did ask him, my last question before leaving, and he answered with as terse a "no" as I'd ever heard. It was his final word on that, or any, subject, as he chose to walk away from me. The man was sensitive about his gorillas.

The Olds was going against the stream. At four o'clock everyone tries to leave the financial district. I parked in a garage near the Standard Oil Building. I was running late, and it didn't help that Walter's office was a security building. Visitation approval took another five minutes. When I met Terrance Walters he was looking at his watch and his briefcase. It was 4:10.

"I had allotted you fifteen minutes, Mr. Winter. You've used ten."

Terrence Walters was a small man, well dressed and well groomed. His suit jacket was buttoned, and he had a button-down shirt, monogrammed on the cuff. He didn't smile, but still managed to show enough polished teeth to give the impression he had a dentist on retainer. His hair was thinning, but each follicle had its place. He had manicured nails, little white and pink pearls on dovish hands that were never offered my way.

I didn't make a point of offering my hand, either. I took up a few more of his precious seconds by looking around the office. It was adorned tastefully. There were some nice, subdued paintings, a few antique clocks, and a few framed diplomas. All of the paper clips on his desk were stored in a receptacle, and the pens were neatly lined up. There was an aura of respectability everywhere. Maybe that's why I doubted him.

It's said in every fat person there's a thin person screaming to come out. There wasn't any conscious reason to think it, but in Terrence Walters I sensed something dirty screaming to come out. Or be kept in.

"Five minutes should be enough, Mr. Walters," I said, "for now. I've a few questions for you. Some or none of them might be pertinent to Anita's disappearance. Right now I'm doing a lot of fishing."

"Go ahead."

"How'd you get along with your daughter?"

"She was away at school most of her life. I think that prevented us from being very close."

"When did she first go away?"

"When she was six."

"But she was home summers and holidays?"

"Mostly, yes."

"Mostly?"

"She started going to school year around."

"At what age?"

"Twelve."

"Is that usual for the deaf?"

"Anita decided that she needed the extra schooling."

Walters never hurried his speech. He reminded me of a lawyer—which he was—but it was more than that. He was too careful with his words, talked in what I like to call "adulterer's speech." At some point in their life some people purposely lose the capacity for verbal spontaneity. Some do it to maintain the veneer of the person they've chosen to create. For others there's the necessity of sifting through a sheaf of stories and lies to find the appropriate answer. My job was to listen to Walter's answers and hear the echoes behind them.

"Did you ever visit Anita at Greenmont?"

"I'm a very busy man."

"Did you?"

"No."

"Do you love Anita?"

"I don't like your line of questioning, Mr. Winter. And I don't see how this will help you in your search."

"I still have two minutes by your timepiece, Mr. Walters. I'd like you to answer the question."

"Yes. I love Anita."

"What do you know about her life."

"What kind of a question is that?"

"One that I'd like you to answer."

"I obviously know many things about my daughter's life. I know she's a model. I know she loves animals . . ."

"How do you know these things? Do you know sign language?"

"Not really."

"So how do you know these things?"

"Mostly my wife keeps me up to date."

"Did Anita talk with you?"

"Of course."

"How? And when?"

"She called sometimes."

I looked pointedly at his phone. It wasn't a TDD. A TDD wouldn't have fit in with the decor.

"She called home," he said.

"How often?"

"Every few weeks."

"Did she love you?"

"Of course."

"Of course? A father who can't even communicate with his daughter? A father who doesn't visit? What does that say to you?"

"It says that I'm very busy. It says that you lose skills if you don't constantly practice."

I still couldn't open him up. He was the unflappable lawyer who birthed every word with a cautious heritage.

"I understand Anita hated you."

"And where did you hear this?"

"One of her teachers told me."

"That's news to me."

"Why would she tell that to a teacher?"

"I don't know. Maybe because I gave her an Audi instead of a BMW for her sixteenth birthday."

"Why was she angry?"

"Who says she was?"

"Just about everyone I talked to. They say her anger began to surface when she was sixteen."

"Isn't that the usual age?"

"I wouldn't call her anger usual."

"What would you call it?"

"Long-consuming."

Walters looked at his watch. It agreed with the antique clocks. The interview had gone for three minutes too long.

"I have an appointment, Mr. Winter. I would suggest punctuality next time."

He gestured with his hand. I decided to leave. Walters saw me to the elevator, but didn't take it down with me. Which was just as well. I spoke to the four walls. "Son of a bitch."

I called the operator, who teletyped Ellen, who talked with me. It was a merry mess I guessed we could grow used to. We debated pasta or Chinese, and made the operator hungry. The Orient won, but there was a spumoni compromise.

Ellen agreed to drive into the City and meet me at the Hunan on Kearney St. I got there early to claim a table. It's probably the most popular hole-in-the-wall restaurant in the world. Success had dictated a new and larger clone on Sansome, where the food was just as good, but I liked the cramped atmosphere of the original Hunan. I was sure Ellen would like it, also. The din and clatter were part of the place, a part she'd miss, but the better part was the smell and taste of the food.

She arrived with a breathless "Hello," followed by "What smells so great?" She proved a woman after my own heart, and got down to the serious business of looking at the menu right away. We agreed to share soup, appetizers, and entrees, and quickly decided on sweet-and-sour and Won ton, pot stickers and barbecued ribs, and kung pao chicken. The last entree was debated. She wanted Mongolian beef. I wanted the harvest pork with the bean sauce. We settled on the Hunan beef and clicked beer bottles. Then I presented her with three napkins.

"Why the napkins?" she asked.

"Winter's theory of a good Chinese restaurant," I said. "If your nose isn't running, if your eyes don't tear some, the food's no good."

The food was good, everything that I promised, three napkins and more. We ate with chopsticks, and even with those wooden obstacles the food disappeared quickly. Finally we came up for air.

"T.G.I.F.," I said.

"What do you usually do on Fridays?" she asked.

"Call Dial-A-Prayer."

"Really."

"Call Audubon's rare bird alert number."

"What's that?"

"528-0288."

"Quit teasing. What is it?"

"Bird-sighting recording. Tells you what and where and when. And now you're going to ask, 'why?' "

"You're really a bird watcher?"

"Yes. Now and again. Maybe one day I'll be confident enough to announce myself as an amateur ornithologist."

"How often do you go out?"

"Not as often as I'd like."

I didn't mean to be defensive, and she didn't mean to pry, but it seemed as if we were guilty of both. It was the new awkward stage, there because our intimacy had preceded our knowing each other. Our minds had to do the fancy footwork to catch up to where our bodies had been. I picked up a piece of kung pao chicken with the chopsticks and made the offering to her mouth. She accepted, and reciprocated. We vied with each other to find the tastiest remaining morsels, and found the greater pleasure in the giving and not the taking. With Hunan food, that says a lot.

"So did you go birding last week? That's what they say, isn't it? Birding?"

"Yes, that's what they say. And no, I didn't. I was on a different hunt."

She encouraged me with a craned neck.

"I was on a surveillance last week. It was the kind of case I didn't want to take, but it involved a friend of a friend of a friend."

The craned neck asked for more. I don't deny fine necks and birds, usually in that order.

"Many times people call private investigators with their life's problems. They think that somehow we can help. And that's wrong."

"But you did help?"

"I was lucky."

"Tell me."

I sighed, but she couldn't hear sighs, so I talked.

"Six months ago an assailant stripped, beat, and abused a woman in her own house. He did everything but rape her. And he told her he would be back one night soon to do that.

"The woman was terrified. She went to the police. And after taking the report they couldn't do anything but offer coffee and professional sympathy.

"The woman was a little unbalanced from the assault, and a lot scared. Her world, all the big and little in it, seemed turned against her. Strangers were enemies, and friends weren't the same. And then the terror started, and I guess that made her a little more unbalanced.

"Her assailant came back. Several times. She once saw him across the street. He just stood and waved.

"Another time he came to the door. She had a peephole. He stood there and told her he was selling magazines, and held up one of those supposed true crime ones, with the banner headlines about dismemberments.

"The next time she saw him was midnight. She hadn't been bothered in more than a month and was beginning to think her horror was over. She was asleep on the second floor when something awakened her. There wasn't anyone in the room. There wasn't anything to make her believe anything was wrong, except . . .

"A tapping. Not a constant tapping, not a regular tapping, but a tap, and then a long pause, or several, and another tap. The noise was coming from a downstairs window.

"Her first impulse was to call the police, but she didn't. By this time she knew they thought her a kook and a nuisance. So she listened, and every so often she heard the sound. It could be a bird, she decided, or some animal, or a loose shutter. It could be a lot of things. So she went downstairs, and every now and again there was that tap. Tap. Tap.

"She approached that window. There wasn't any way to

look out to what was making the noise except by opening the curtain. She reached out. Tap. And when she opened the curtains, he was there. And he wagged his fingers from his ears, and stuck out his tongue, and made a horrible face.

"She screamed to wake the dead. He liked that. He fed on her terror, fed on that power of making her believe in the bogey man, and the devil, and how there's no God above to help, there's just him, the master. When the woman told me her story, I believed her. I couldn't disbelieve her terror. So I said those words a private investigator shouldn't, because usually he can't: 'I'll help.' "

"But you said you did help."

"I was lucky. I waited ten nights. How many people do you think have that kind of money?"

"She was rich?"

"No. I didn't charge her. How could I? She was just a victim. But a private investigator doesn't make a living by giving away professional favors. And usually you don't take a case because it can be solved. Just about everything can be solved, but can you afford the time?"

"No sermonizing before you finish the story."

"On the tenth night he showed up. And I caught him."

"That's all?"

"He's in jail now. But he'll get a good lawyer who will point out that he never committed any physical rape. And the same lawyer will present the questionable mental history of my client and make her credibility suspect."

"Will he harass her again when he's released?"

"I don't think so. I think he lost his taste for terror."

I picked up my bottle and took a long pull. It didn't quite wash the taste out of my mouth. I had consulted Norman Cohen on the case, and he had given me a personality profile of who and what the terrorist was, and how and why he got his jollies. But the larger part of our discussion centered on the fastest and most permanent way of reforming our man, a way short of murder, not that that option wasn't discussed. I heard the kind of therapy shrinks never prescribe.

And when I did get my hands on him, I practiced without a license for the better part of an hour. First he pled with me, and then with God, and then there was only his begging, and the smell of fear, and his incontinence. I left him with my card, and the vow that I would kill him if he ever played his games again.

"Hey," said Ellen. She reached out a hand and touched mine. I returned her squeeze.

"Did you enjoy?"

The waiter hovered over us. He smiled at our hand-holding. Servers always like blooming love. It usually makes for bigger tips. We voiced our satisfaction, rubbing our tummies in a pantomime for further show.

"Very good," he said. His accent was that of someone not long in this country. He presented us with the bill and fortune cookies. The Chinese have always known how to combine the bitter with the sweet.

"You pick," I said.

Ellen chose the cookie the farthest away from her. Human nature. The fortune cookie is always greener on the other side. I took the hand fate dealt me. Mine read: Paris is the San Francisco of Europe.

"Let's trade," she said.

We switched the slips. Ellen's read: Romantic Prospects Are Near.

"I don't like yours as much as mine," said Ellen.

"That's the way the fortune cookie crumbles."

"I still don't like it," she said.

"Complain directly to the source," I said. "There is a little fortune cookie factory not too far from here."

"Where?"

"Near the spumoni. Let's go."

We took a bus to North Beach, and then backtracked a

little by walking over to Cadell Place. It's a little alley that few people would walk up without a reason. We had a reason. Ellen noticed the smell first. She could have led, could have floated in the air on the aromatic trail, but followed me to a little doorfront.

I opened the door and gave a big smile. Three old Chinese women looked up. It wasn't Willy Wonka's factory, but it was unique. We walked down some steps into an honest-to-goodness mini-fortune cookie factory. Bags and bags of the cookies took up most of the room. We did a lot of watching and smelling. A little conveyor belt sent the hot cookie dough along the line. A machine crimped the dough into the characteristic seashell forms, and the women made sure the fortunes were inserted. I liked the last part, liked the idea that little hands inserted the fates instead of machinery.

The Chinese women didn't speak any English, but Ellen understood their gestures very well. They were proud of their little room and its wares. We were treated to some broken fortune cookies, and after bowing our thanks made our exit.

Arm in arm we walked around North Beach. In my mind North Beach is synonymous with pasta and sleaze and freaks, in that order, but increasingly I find those are just memories. The Italian accents on the streets, the staccato arguments that sound like opera intrigue, are fewer and fewer. Now the accents are urbane, or Cantonese. No bene. No goddamn bene.

The avant-garde made their stand in North Beach in the fifties and sixties, brought with them their poetry and music, but those are now things of the past. A few husks remain, the City Lights Bookstore and Vesuvio Cafe, but the happening is now somewhere else. The gypsies and street jesters moved on to a place where a cup of joe doesn't cost three dollars, and where herbal tea doesn't go for more than herbal smoke.

With the older Italians dying, and their children living in duplexes on the peninsula, the rich, and the Chinese who have pooled their money together to collectively become the rich, have taken over. Favorite stores and restaurants are going, going, gone. Even the flesh dens, the Condor Clubs and Big Al's, are pale versions of what they were. When clip-and-strip joints become sanitized, they should close their doors.

Supposedly Ellen and I were looking for spumoni, but it proved to be a hunt for another Grail. My spumoni spot was closed, and I didn't want to settle for frozen yogurt. We passed by Finocchio's, where packed houses have watched female impersonators for close to half a century. Columnist Herb Caen once noted, "Joe Finocchio lives off the labor of his fruits."

North Beach is North Beach, but on a summer weekend night, a tourist night, it wasn't where we wanted to be, so we kept walking. It was a beautiful night, and our feet weren't feeling the steps, so we covered a lot of ground. Walking and talking with a deaf person is not the easiest endeavor, so mostly we just touched and smiled. We decided on a nightcap near where we had started the evening at a lounge on Kearney. It was pricey, and glitzy, and made me long for Cookie's Star Buffet, another good bar that was now gone. I didn't tell Ellen about Cookie's. She was too young, or I was too old. I was grateful the new bar didn't put an umbrella in my Scotch. Ellen and I didn't talk much. The place was too dark for her to lip read, and I was too tired to say anything anyway. We finished our drinks and walked outside.

"Where'd you park?" I asked.

"Is the night over?"

"Yes."

She mentioned a garage, then shut her mouth. She was upset, and I didn't feel very tolerant. We walked toward the garage, our steps too quick, so I stopped her with my hands.

"I'm tired, okay? It was a long day, and tomorrow will be, too. I'd like to invite you over to my place, and I'd like to snuggle with you, but I need a rain check. Okay?"

"Okay," she said.

For a short time we walked more easily, but I ruined things by opening my mouth. I didn't say anything, but I moved my lips while trying to remember some words. Ellen noticed.

"I didn't catch that," she said.

"I didn't say anything. I was just trying to remember a line from Shakespeare. It seemed appropriate for the day."

"Which line?"

"An ape's an ape, a varlet's a varlet, whether clad in silk or scarlet."

"Why that line?"

"I talked with a varlet today," I said, "and an ape. I much preferred the latter."

"They have to do with Anita?"

"Right."

A flush came to Ellen's face. "Why does everyone have to be so obsessed with Anita? Why do *you* have to be?"

I was surprised at her anger. I didn't have a ready answer, and Ellen didn't seem to want to wait for one. We reached the garage, and she said good-bye without looking at me. I watched her present her stub at the window. An attendant went off to get her car.

She kept her back turned to me, so I never had a chance to tell her good-night.

11

THE PHONE RANG IN the middle of a good dream, and I felt warm and didn't want to be disturbed, so I let it ring knowing Miss Tuntland would probably pick it up on the fifth or sixth summons, but she didn't. I finally reached for it.

"This is Winter."

"And this is not your wake up service. Or at least it shouldn't be."

"Good morning, Miss Tuntland."

"It's ten-thirty. It's edging towards afternoon. I thought there was a certain exhibition you were going to today."

"There is. I am."

There was enough drill sergeant in her voice to get me to sit up straight.

"I happen to know that Vincent's speaking at the museum at one," she said. "Even the *Chron* knows that. Hold on, I've got a call."

I was glad for the reprieve. Her other call gave me time to rub my eyes, scratch around, and yawn. She came back on the line.

"Hello."

"Who was that?" I asked, already beginning to strip.

"Just another one of my eccentric clients."

"Another one?"

"You heard me."

"What's he or she do for a living?"

"He. And that's privileged information."

"You're beginning to sound like a doctor. So the investigator in me would guess that your client is probably a doctor."

"Sorry, Sherlock. I've had that pleasure. The calls always come at the worst times. And the doctors think they're God, not the son of, just God. And they always pay late. No, thank you. Having a doctor for a client violates my first rule."

"And what violates your second?"

"Having a private detective."

"Should I ask about your third rule?"

"Doing extra work for clients."

"I'm glad you don't consider our little enterprises extra . . ."

"Donuts and Things."

"What?"

"On Polk. That was the tip from my client. He told me he was meeting his friend there tomorrow, and also told me that they make the best doughnuts in San Francisco. I want, oh, two or three, no, make that four. I'll skip my dinner salad. And surprise me with a variety."

"You're an extortionist."

"I know Vincent's real name."

"Donuts and Things," I said outloud, writing the name down.

"Neal Patchen," she said, as I continued to write, "a.k.a. 'Real Passion.' He actually used that one for a while in his experimental days, and the skinny is he lived up to it. On and off the canvas. Neal's from Arizona. He had his bohemian days, but he never came close to being a starving artist. His parents are well off, father a developer or something like that."

"What should I know about his art?"

"What you'd expect from any artist that's about forty. A lot of stages."

"Tell me about them."

"He sold his first paintings during his 'Real Passion' days, twenty years ago. He was sort of an obscene Peter Max. Then he became serious, didn't sign his works 'Real Passion.' Signed them 'Patchen.' Those were his Jackson Pollack and sand days, spent mostly in Santa Fe. He lived in an adobe home. Mixed paints and sand on his canvas. Mixed drugs, too. Made some pottery. And then left Santa Fe to do some traveling."

"How much drugs and how much traveling?"

"A lot and a lot. He toured the world on high octane."

"And today?"

"Espresso is supposed to be his drug of choice. And San Francisco is his roost."

"Lucky us."

"It took him a long time to find his muse. For a while his work was sort of surrealistic, then he started doing a variety of stuff, some modern, some impressionistic, and a lot of object art. About ten years ago he changed his name to Vincent. Everyone guesses the name comes from Vincent Van Gogh, but our Vincent doesn't talk about it."

I scratched at my notes until I was satisfied, then asked, "Do you still want to defend him from my slurs?"

Miss Tuntland was quiet for a time. "He's not a Boy Scout," she finally said, "but it's hard telling truth from fiction. Sometimes artists act the way they do to get a name. If they're outrageous enough, maybe their works will be noticed."

"And what did Vincent do to get his name?"

"When he was Real Passion he had a unique way of signing his paintings. He ejaculated into a cup and mixed his semen with red paint. He said that made his signature a living thing, and added a primal nature to his work. A 'modern fertility rite' he called it."

I made a despairing sound. "What else?"

"He gave a demonstration once during his sand-and-paint days. he cut himself, quite deeply, and let his blood mix with the paint. Said that you had to give of your life fluid to create. That caused quite a stir."

"Maybe I ought to hold court while I shave."

Miss Tuntland rightfully ignored me. "Object art allowed him, and continues to allow, his displays of fancy. Skeletons doing housework. Feathered model airplanes. Paintings that deserve hanging at Madame Tussaud's. His stuff isn't background, and neither is the artist."

"Which means?"

"Which means that while his reputation has grown, so has his penchant for playing a larger-than-life figure. He's dressed in black for the last six years and likes capes. Being the center of attention says it mildly. Center of the world would be more to his liking."

"He's a jerk, isn't he, Miss Tuntland?"

"Yes, Mr. Winter, but a very talented one."

"I can hear him talking to himself in the morning: 'To be a poseur or a genius? That's the poser.' "

"Maybe he needs to be both."

"Shakespeare needed you buzzing in his ear, Miss Tuntland. And I need you like . . ."

"A doughnut needs its hole."

"Exactly so."

I gave a twenty to a neighborhood kid to get the doughnuts and make the delivery. My revenge on Miss Tuntland was that instead of getting just four doughnuts, I told the kid to get a dozen, "and make 'em the gooey type, with fudge, and jimmies, and double glaze." Miss Tuntland, like most women, said she constantly had to be on the watch for calories. Now there was a lot for her to watch. And probably sample. I wasn't worried about her curses. Incantations don't work with a full mouth.

It was Saturday, but I knew Leland sometimes put in extra hours at the library. Saving old and precious books was a labor of love for him. He truly believed future generations would one day appreciate his paper prizes, even if the present one didn't. He fought the bureaucrats who tried to cut his funding, but mostly he fought the elements and the pressing forces of passing days. He worked against time, a Quixotic battle, but one he never conceded. As the self-appointed guardian of the books, Leland was expert at rebinding texts, and patching paper. He railed at the chemicals twentieth-century publishers used in their paper, said that most books had a thirty-year-self-destruct clock, and that it was only his elixirs and remedies that extended their lives. It's Leland's belief that libraries stand between humanity and the Dark Ages, and are the bastions of light in a confused age. I never argued the point, just regularly stopped by for my dose of light.

The library was on the way to the museum. I wandered up to the third floor, stuck my nose in Special Collections, and asked if Leland was in. He heard my voice and came out from the back room, his expression sad. He was, he informed me, patching a "horribly mistreated first edition of *Madame Bovary.*"

"Flaubert can wait," I said. "There's an exhibition at the Museum of Modern Art that you might like. It promises to be a study in perversity."

Leland said something no doubt profound in French that concluded with "mon ami." It was almost enough to make me reconsider my invitation.

The San Francisco Museum of Modern Art is located in the War Memorial Veterans Building. We entered the museum from Van Ness. It's located on the top floor, a big enough floor not only for Picasso's and Klee's, but also for some of the artists of the Bay Area. Not that Vincent was being touted as some local yokel with a paintbrush. He was beyond that, past the emerging stage, into the "if not a great, then close enough" category. His works were considered a major display of a living artist, an honor usually given to the half-dead. A marquee announced the Vincent exhibition. I paid for the two of us at the door and was given a brochure. The cover page showed Vincent working at an easel. It was a close shot, and didn't clue people in to the background clutter.

"Where to now?" asked Leland.

"I'm tempted to wander around the museum," I said, "but I'm going to have to concentrate on the Vincent exhibit. It involves a case."

"On-the-job culture."

I pointed dubiously to one of Vincent's sculptures, something that looked like a multicolored anemone. "Yeah. The kind of culture they take at a free clinic."

Lee gave an exasperated flip of his shoulder and proceeded forward without me. Three large rooms had been set aside for the exhibition. A sign above the doorway to the first room read: VINCENT: THE EARLY YEARS. There were no naked baby pictures, but there were some of his Real Passion and Patchen works, and a retrospective of the times that produced them. Neither semen nor bloodletting was mentioned. Thank the Lord for little favors.

Vincent's early pieces were colorful and chock full of messages, none of them exactly subtle. The libidinous and the oppressed played and raged, sometimes even in the same painting. I compared his titles with his paintings, and they were just as blunt. 'Satyriasis' was accurate, as was 'Raging Slaves' and 'Primal Dance,' which probably explained why I liked his pottery best. It looked functional and wasn't gaudy, and there were no messages as far as I could see. As for his signatures on the clay, I wasn't about to have them analyzed. That might have given a whole new meaning to sperm banks.

Vincent's Santa Fe days weren't exactly Zane Gray, but the sand was real and the colors were desert genuine. I liked them fine for what they were: Heinz 57 on display. They were a gentler Vincent, and didn't prepare me for the next room, which the entry sign announced as EVOLV-ING VINCENT.

He hadn't been idle during his touring and drugging days. He was a prolific sponge, capturing and releasing a lot of styles on canvas. If there was any continuity, any tradition, in his works, it was seen in the loudness of his colors, even if his weaponry evolved from bazooka to Gatling gun. Vincent began putting subthemes in his paintings, background images that went beyond pelvic thrusts and worlds of madness. He started getting more complex, richer, busier. There was a lot going on in his paintings, and Vincent was ironic, even sardonic, in a lot of his works. He had two identical paintings, one titled 'Sunset in Hell' and the other 'Sunset in Heaven.' In both it looked like a Howard Johnson's was sinking off into the horizon.

The third and largest Vincent room featured his art from the last ten years, art for the most part that amused and terrified. In his 'Cheep Milk' birds mooed, while 'Purrafornaila' featured cats purring as they chewed human fingers. 'Walkers On Parade' showed an unfortunate group of geriatrics and their ambulatory equipment prom-enading in the style of the 'Spirit of '76.' Lee chose that moment to return to my side. He had evidently decided that this was art you didn't have to talk about in hushed tones.

"Join the parade?" he asked.

"Come to think of it," I said, "the last time I saw fig-ures like these was at the 'Gay Pride Parade.' "

Lee stepped lively, imaginary baton in hand, and marched over to where Vincent's paintings were featured. I pretended I didn't know him.

Vincent's body of work convinced me he had talent, a conclusion I came to begrudgingly. But I also thought it was a talent he misused. From a technical sense I admired 'A Widow.' The shadows were provocative, and blended wonderfully with the colors for a dream effect. They made as sultry a woman in oil as any painter has ever done, which was all the more the pity. What could have been a great painting was ruined by Vincent's willful desire to shock. He didn't want to show you the electrical socket, he wanted you to put your finger in it.

At first glance, maybe even second, nothing was wrong. The pure sensuousness of the painting held you. You didn't question it. You experienced it. You were first person, present tense. With an exclamation point.

The foreground featured the parlor, and an opened bottle of red wine. The seats looked comfortable, but the woman wasn't sitting down. Reclined in a corner, her back against a wall, she was naked. A sheen of sweat covered her body. She waited, and her desire was yours. Paintings don't usually make your legs weak. They have to be special to draw your face closer, and make you think, make you remember. Vincent had painted a dream, the kind of dream you can never quite remember.

But the closer I examined the painting, the more something disturbed me. I wanted to ignore the bells and whistles, to take in the attraction without question, to accept physically without mind, but Vincent didn't allow that. He included enough hints to turn the viewer cold after the hot. Was that hair, or something else, something gossamer and threadlike, even weblike, all over her head? And what was in the shadows of her bent arms, and spread legs? Just a reflection, or another set of arms and legs? And her eyes, what kind of desire was there? Carnal certainty, but something more. When I looked closely I could see her pubic area was not quite right, not the black triangle I expected, but a red hourglass.

Vincent used his paintings like a carny barker. He drew you in, then he gulled you. Sometimes he just made you laugh, albeit shakily. One picture was entitled 'The Plastic Surgeon's Mistress.' A circus backdrop, but in the foreground a woman is chained to a revolving platform. Blood flows down her leg, courtesy of her husband's cutlery. At her feet a pool of blood has formed. The knifethrowing husband, the cuckold, holds another knife in hand. He knows the truth, and she knows he knows, but the ritual isn't concluded. They stare eye to eye, and it's hard to tell which looks more uncertain, which feels the cutting edge of despair more. He knows his misses send his Mrs. to her lover, for professional services and otherwise. And she knows how the steel can cut, how it can kill. The audience looks very pleased. They're ready to cheer wherever the next knife lands.

I decided I didn't want to be part of the audience, and kept walking. Vincent was as prolific as he was disturbing. 'I Need Her' showed a naked woman being kneaded and molded into something else by two strong male hands. The pubic hairs looked real, and so did the flesh, the flesh being rolled like dough. The only vague part was what the woman was being kneaded into. Maybe sweet buns.

The next painting, 'Looking for a Drain,' wasn't so vague. I gave it a cursory glance, then came back to it. The picture showed a man with an opened mouth. On top of his forehead, and jutting out of the painting, was a faucet handle. By description it matched the handle that Anita Walters had needed replaced in her apartment. What had been her cabinet door was now hinged to a canvas titled 'Opening Doors.' I looked at both paintings for a while, and wondered if they were signatures to a murder.

A figure approached behind me. "Haven't you had enough of the good-housekeeping section?" he asked.

"Only if you've tired of ogling nudes. I saw you drooling over there."

"They're not traditional nudes," said Leland. "You just have to look a little closer to see that."

"Oh?"

"Like this one."

I glanced at a pen drawing of a naked man, then looked back to Leland.

"His equipment," said Lee, "isn't normal. It's a pen."

I looked at the genitalia, then searched the title of the painting. It was THE PEN IS MIGHTIER THAN THE SWORD. But the space between the words "Pen" and "Is" was barely a space at all.

"Let's go hear Vincent talk," I said. "I've seen enough to make me *pen*sive."

The auditorium was overflowing, so Lee and I stood in the back. Vincent didn't have much of a prepared speech, but used significant pauses to precede theatrical lines. He narrated a slide show of his works, and used a flip chart to make some points, but I was disappointed that he didn't open his veins. In the two days since I had last seen him, he hadn't managed to lose his tic. I wondered if he had adopted the mannerism purposely, like his black clothes. It was an effective attention getter. The man thrived on being different, on drawing notice to his person. Ten minutes into Vincent's talk, Leland whispered to me that library duty called, and I rather enviously watched him leave.

Vincent finally opened the floor to questions, which gave him a chance to pontificate even more. Most of the crowd ate up his pabulum, and for the better part of two hours he held his position at the lectern. Then there were five minutes of thank you's directed at the great man, and a chance for him to hold court with all his admirers afterwards. I waited on the fringe. Vincent saw me, but made no acknowledgment. When most of the faithful had finally left, I approached him, and this time he met my eyes.

"Ah, yes, Mr . . . ?"

"Winter, Mr. Patchen, Stuart Winter."

"How may Vincent help you, Mr. Winter?"

"Two of your paintings interested me, Mr. Patchen."

His black cape ruffled some, and his eyes turned mean and uneasy.

"And which two paintings are those?"

" 'Looking For a Drain' and 'Opening Doors.' "

He gave a benign smile to his lingering followers that didn't look totally phony. "Vincent likes those two, also, Mr. Winter."

"Don't mistake me, Mr. Patchen," I said. "I didn't say I liked them. I said they interested me. Why don't you tell me about them?"

"Is that a roundabout way of asking Vincent where he obtained the spigot, or whatever it is, and the cabinet door?"

"Yes."

"Vincent tore them from Anita's apartment. Probably half a dozen people saw Vincent do it. Vincent can supply their names if you'd like. Vincent was inspired to create and needed those objects."

"Do you often go around ripping things off their hinges?"

"Only when necessary, Mr. Winter. Only when necessary."

I asked him for the names of the witnesses, and by the reaction of his disciples, I blasphemed. They didn't understand what was going on, only knew that my manner was offensive. But Vincent was forgiving. He gave me the names, then added, "They will also tell you that Vincent paid Anita for the damages."

"How much?"

"A hundred dollars, two hundred. Vincent doesn't remember."

"Thank you, Mr. Patchen."

I drank four glasses of Scotch in about forty minutes. Mal didn't question my thirst. He was unobtrusive, gliding in with the Glenfiddich, and lingering for that extra moment to see if I wanted to talk. I didn't, not yet. I was early, and needed the extra time and drinks before Norman arrived. My pewter mug felt good in my hand. It was antique, had somehow survived the Revolutionary War. Probably a Tory had owned it, I thought, a Tory who wouldn't give it up for the bullets of a new nation. You start thinking like that after four quick drinks.

There was a method to my madness, and I wasn't exactly new to it. Some cases don't allow you to just go through the motions, and this was one of those cases. I had to walk with it, and work with it, and think with it. And now I was going to get drunk with it. Victor Hugo was my inspiration. Hugo had written about drink in *Les Misérables,* had written about the four goblets that lined a wall, and the inscriptions upon them. The first was monkey wine; the second, lion wine; the third, sheep wine; and the last, swine wine. The animals marked man's descending degrees of drunkenness. I was at the Edinburgh Castle ready to oink in swine wine, in search of a dirty drunk so that I could think dirty thoughts. It wasn't scientific, but sometimes it worked.

I was at least halfway to my wallow when Norman joined me. Like Mal, he didn't question my need for the drinks. He just attempted to keep up. He was on his swine wine glass when he started talking freely, complaining too loudly that the wine was no good.

"So don't order wine in a Scotch bar," I told him again. The same advice had been given on his monkey, lion, and sheep glasses.

Norman wagged his finger at me. "I don't know why you always bring me here," he said. "It's antique, like your drink. Who drinks Scotch now-a-days?"

He raised himself from his barstool and started to walk toward the bathroom. He was a little unsteady, but cloven hooves do that to you.

It was Saturday at the Edinburgh Castle, a night I usually avoided. Tourist night, gawk at the bagpiper, throw some inaccurate darts. But even on its worst night the Castle is San Francisco's best bar. Model airplanes and jets hang from the ceiling, and Winston Churchill busts stare at you from amidst countless labels of Scotch. A suspicious parrot, with the same Churchill stare, and same first name, rested in the corner. Winston rarely squawked, never spoke, and wasn't very good about accepting new fingers. He had grown to accept mine. By standing tradition I didn't drink until Winston came over to have his head scratched, and luckily he hadn't kept me waiting tonight. Sometimes the bird wasn't so cooperative, but a good Scotch doesn't worry about a little extra aging. The mugs of the regulars hung on the racks, each one distinctive. My pewter mug wasn't as flashy as most, had in fact a tarnished exterior, but its interior was whistle clean from a Scotch finish. The mug's wear showed it had served other hands well. It hadn't done too badly in my own either.

I don't know whether I took my office on Geary because of the Castle's proximity, but I was glad it was nearby. I doubted there was a bar west of Edinburgh with more brands of Scotch. It didn't boast much in the way of food, but the fish and chips were good, even if they arrived cold more often than not. The bar had an iffy exterior on the eerie side of Geary. From the outside no one could ever guess the size of the place. Its lack of ostentation kept away a crowd I didn't want anyway.

I looked at my reflection, my face showing between the large letters of the mirror that advertised BASS & CO.'S PALE BURTON ALES. The mirror was old, and never gave an accurate reflection, but I could see my pink snout emerging, could feel the little curlicue tail pushing into the barstool beneath me. I was about ready to start talking, theorizing. Hell, I was about ready to start a chorus of "Old MacDonald Had a Scotch Farm."

Norman was about on the same wavelength. He came back singing.

"Another, gentlemen?"

"Thanks, Mal."

"And a coffee with mine," said Norman.

Mal nodded, and fetched our drinks. I watched his face and thought I saw a hint of his small smile. He had been at the Castle for twenty years, and his ears were as good as his hands. Unless you watched him very carefully, you never saw his small smile. He was the officious, anonymous bartender, softspoken and unobtrusive.

It was the right time to talk. I told Norman everything about the case, and in the telling appropriated about a dozen of the Castle's napkins. My entries and diagrams went all around and through the illustration of a Scotty begging at a martini glass. The Castle's napkins are black and red, good tartan colors. My observations were less well defined. Mal kept supplying us with ammunition, and we kept talking. It was almost two o'clock, and we were alone, when Norman crumpled up my napkins and confronted me.

"Okay," he said. "So now I know everything. And that seems to add up to nothing. Right?"

I nodded.

"So we'll play a game. I ask questions, and you give me your first answer."

"Norman . . ."

"Just humor me, would you, Stuart?"

"All right."

"Is Anita alive?"

I gave an answer I didn't want to give. "No."

"Why not?"

"She wouldn't just disappear. That's not her way."

"So who killed her?"

"I'm not sure."

"Who could have killed her?"

"Just about anyone."

"Name the suspects."

"Vincent. Kevin Bateson. Dr. Harrison . . ."

"Why Harrison?"

"I even surprised myself with that name . . ."

"So why'd you say it?"

"Something's being covered up there. I don't know what."

"What do you think?"

"He was bothered?"

"Who was bothered? Dr. Harrison?"

"Yes. And Joseph?"

"Are you asking? Does the gorilla know something?"

"Yeah."

I gave him a hard look, a look to tell this shrink he'd better not say I was crazy, but Norman didn't have that kind of look. He was too busy thinking of other questions.

"Any other suspects?"

"Terrence Walters," I heard myself saying.

"Her father? Are you kidding?"

"No. Just reacting in my gut to something that's wrong there too . . ."

"What's wrong?"

"He didn't, he doesn't, know how to sign. Why would a father not learn his daughter's language? Why would he shut off her world to him?"

"You tell me."

"He didn't want to hear her thoughts. He wanted her . . ."

"He wanted her what?"

"As his own creation. Without an identity, except for the one he gave her. Without words, except those he wanted to hear."

"And what words were those?"

"I'm not sure."

"Really? Or aren't you saying?"

"It's . . ."

"It's what?"

"Farfetched. Probably."

"Farfetched? Or disgusting?"

"Both."

"Say it."

"He molested her?"

"Are you asking or telling?"

"He molested her."

"A respected barrister? A leading citizen?"

"Yes."

"How do you know?"

"Her anger. That explains it. And her behavior."

"Explain."

"Look at the pattern. I don't know why I didn't think about it before. When she was sixteen she began to rebel against authority. She began to realize she had rights. And she also began to realize just how badly she had been abused. But how do you confront a father? It takes some growing before you can do that, some muscles that time and experience provide. So for a time she just avoided him, and took on other authority figures instead. She joined groups, and learned about her rights, and her worth."

"That's not unusual. That doesn't tell me she was abused."

"What about her relationships? Do you remember how cold she was with Darren Fielder? He said she just lay there, and didn't react at all. She knew how to withdraw, knew how to make it not hurt her."

"The young are often confused during their first sexual encounters . . ."

"Bullshit, Norman. What about her behavior toward Will Harrady? She was so desperate for affection. And when he pushed her away she couldn't stand the rejection. She was confused, God, she was confused. Love, father images, what was right, what was wrong—she didn't know what she was doing."

"She knew enough to strike back."

"Yes. Her victim days were over."

"And what does that mean?"

"I think she began to confront a lot of people. It didn't matter whether they were innocent or not. Think of the wounds of her childhood. How do those kinds of wounds usually heal? The scabs don't protect very well."

"Is that what got her killed?"

"I don't know."

He gave me a dubious look.

"I really don't know, Norman."

I was glad I was drunk. I didn't have to feel the implications of everything I was saying. The ache that I'd feel all the way in my bones would come later. I could follow trains of thought that our minds usually derail. Terrence Walters, pinstripe, power broker. Neat, natty, man. Legal mind, legal air, and how, you sonofabitch, you made your daughter despair. I laughed out loud at my rhyme, but Norman didn't notice. I guess he believed in my theory. His head was bent over, his pain not so private. That made me a little mad. I thought shrinks were supposed to be as hardened as private eyes. I thought they had heard it all.

"Don't cry in your wine, Norman," I said. "That's not professional. It's beer you cry in. Don't you ever read Emily Post?"

"Fuck off."

"Hey, Mal! A beer for my friend and me. We need something to cry into!"

"Are you sure, Mr. Winter?"

His words sobered me a little. He'd pour the beer if I asked, even though it was after hours, and past time for him to leave. But his face asked me to reconsider.

"Forget it, Mal. Thanks."

He went back to cleaning his bar. He never left without putting a shine on the fine wood. There were a few spots that didn't have the luster he liked. He worked at them and I watched him for a minute, and felt better for his cleaning, and only wished I could take a towel to my insides, and rub around for a while, and clean away all those dirty things that eat down deep.

"Let's finish our drinks, Norman."

"Make a toast, then," said Norman, his voice not weepy at all, but just a little sad. "Say a toast that gives a little hope to this night, you know, one of your silly, sappy, historical toasts."

"To Andrew Hallidie."

"Explain," he said to my raised glass.

"It's a Scotch bar. He was a Scotsman in San Francisco. In 1869 he saw four horses dragging a cart of passengers up a hill. The horses slipped, and the weight of the cart dragged them down the hill. Like Jack and Jill, but worse. None of the people were hurt, but the horses were. They had to be destroyed.

"That bothered Hallidie. He thought there had to be a more humane way to transport people. And he did something about it. Didn't just talk in a bar, didn't just say 'tsk, tsk,' and wring his hands. He invented the cable car. Without him Tony Bennett wouldn't have had his song, and the City wouldn't be the City."

Norman raised his glass. "To Andrew Hallidie."

We finished our drinks, and said good-night to Mal, who was still working at the last of his spots.

I found Norman a cab. As he got inside he asked me a final question. "Are you sure all the horses had to be killed, Stuart?"

I lied to him, and his question, a question that also asked me whether Anita had to be dead. "No, Norman. I just thought the story sounded better that way."

My office was five blocks away. I don't know what demons prompted me to walk there, but I did. I staggered inside, and even with all the Scotch in my stomach I felt cold. I grabbed an overcoat, and then walked over to my filing cabinet, and took out the Anita Walters file. I only wanted her photo, her pretty face. I talked to her picture for a while, and asked it a lot of questions. And when she didn't answer, I fell dead asleep on my couch.

12

I AWOKE AT ABOUT five a.m. Something disturbed me, some noise I couldn't place—a fact that didn't surprise me in light of all the pounding going on in my head. I tried to look around, but it was hard focusing on a spinning room. It sounded like mail had been dropped through my slot; that I even considered that possibility made me think I was hallucinating. A band marched in my head to the theme "Rest In Peace, Brain Cells." Cottonmouth and throbbing temples drove me to the water cooler and aspirin.

When you still walk unsteadily a few hours after retiring, you know what a serious mistake the night before was. The day wasn't starting too great either. Just making one decision at a time was a monumental task. I was tempted to try to sleep again, but my back started to creak at the sight of my lumpy sofa, and I realized my head wasn't the only part of my body registering complaints, just the loudest. I called for a cab, and when the dispatcher asked me where I was going, I said, "to Never, Never Land," which is probably why I had to walk back up to the office and call again after waiting outside for fifteen minutes. I tripped over a newspaper leaving the room, kicked it out of the way, then went down to wait once more.

It was too early to talk and too early to think. I scuffed my feet on the sidewalk, looked around at the grey and felt the cold, and was sure the outside and my inside were one.

A garbage truck went by, a private one, out to clean somewhere in the City.

All garbage collectors are members of the Scavengers' Protective Association, a very strong, and very unusual, union. It's almost an Italian fraternal organization—no, not even Italian, but more regionalized, Genoese, or Genovese as they call themselves. Long ago the Genovese gave up their fishing nets to ply a new trade, and now more than ever they take their trash seriously. The word is they've found more money in prospecting garbage than any fortyniner ever found in gold.

My cabbie arrived. He was into yawning, and I joined him in that conversation. I gave him the destination for home, sweet, home. I live on Potrero Hill. San Franciscans are very possessive about their hills. There is an ongoing argument as to how many there are in the City. The figures range from forty-seven to fifty-one. You pay to be a billygoat, even on Potrero Hill, a mixed neighborhood, a working class neighborhood that's trying to remain that way. My domicile is a subdivided house, older, but not quite antique, not pretty Victorian like some of my neighbors' dwellings. The cabbie dropped me off, and we each gave the other a final yawn. But my mouth deceived my brain. Sleep wouldn't come, and a cognac helper was out of the question, so I read for a bit, leafing through a few of the books and articles Leland had selected. One article about the deaf population on Martha's Vineyard particularly interested me. In the seventeenth century several of the Vineyard's original settlers had been deaf, and had passed on their disability to their children. Large families were the rule, and with a limited gene pool on the island the deafness was perpetuated throughout the eighteenth and nineteenth centuries.

The Vineyarders had little commerce with the outside world. They developed their own traditions, and made unique solutions to their problems. Being a closed community, they weren't aware that pervasive deafness was un-common. They didn't know it was usually the deaf who had to fit in, and accommodate to a hearing world. So they came upon the natural solution that one old timer voiced: "Everyone here spoke sign language."

The deaf were such an integral part of the community that at town meetings a hearing person signed to keep the deaf informed. Sign language was also used by fishermen. Over howling seas, over blowing winds where shouts wouldn't carry, men signed to one another. But as the hereditary deafness gradually disappeared, as islanders began to marry off-islanders, so too did people lose their finger tongue, even if not completely. The author discovered that some of the older families still used sign language, even though they didn't know it. They unconsciously signed, and in many cases were unconsciously understood.

One older man lamented that sometimes he knew he was signing, or making movements that meant something, but that the person he was talking to had no idea what he was saying with his hands. In my own limited experience with the deaf I had seen that. When they spoke, their hands often moved. It probably wasn't too different from my feeble Spanish. When in doubt, I always interjected English.

I finished with the article, and then started reading the gorilla logs, but something bothered me. I couldn't place my discomfort. Aspirin and warm milk couldn't get the thought out, and the gorilla papers didn't add any illumination to my mental thrashings. I finally fell asleep. When I awoke I was sweating and tossing, and remembering a dream that opened eyes and daylight couldn't put to rest.

I was in front of the Opera House, walking again toward the Museum of Modern Art. I heard a clacking, and I was afraid to turn, but finally did. And there was Anita. She was opening and closing her mouth, clacking her teeth in her struggle to speak, but I couldn't understand what she was saying. She grew impatient with me, upset by my inability to make sense of her talk, and started shaking me. I apologized to her, repeatedly, but it didn't help me understand.

Then she walked away. I tried catching up with her, but she always managed to stay ahead, so I called for her to stop, but of course she couldn't hear me. And now it was my turn to grow frustrated, to curse, and rant, and waste my breath. Anita crossed the street, and I couldn't follow. The traffic kept me from her. So there on the corner I began screaming for an answer from her.

"Who murdered you?"

A hearing person probably couldn't have heard over the noise on the street, but something connected us. Anita turned to me, and we really looked at each other for the first time. She was as pretty as everyone said, and the tragedies in her life only added to her beauty. Speech would have been impossible over the traffic, but she didn't try speech. She signed to me, signed to me her murderer's name. But still I couldn't understand.

I mimicked her signs, tried to understand the pattern of her moving fingers. To someone else they might have meant something—to me they were just moving symbols of my frustration. I had an answer at my fingertips but didn't know what it was.

"Tell me," I said, and I think I was crying, and that's when I heard Anita talk. It was as if she were next to me, by my side, on the street, and in my bed.

"I have," she said.

It was the Sabbath, and I was a practicing pantheist. I called my bird number, then headed south in the Olds, and got off at the Dumbarton Bridge. Coyote Hills is known for its Indian shell mounds. Four thousand years of shucking oysters left an abundance of remains, visible clues of ancient lives, though at the moment, I was more interested in a modern life. Or death. I thought about my dream, of not being able to communicate with Anita. Norman probably would have read a lot of significance into it, finding symbolism and archetypes and a deeper meaning than mere frustration. I was reminded of the Biblical story of Nimrod the great hunter, and his Tower of Babel. Nimrod had thought he could build a castle to the heavens. His prideful act angered Jehovah, who cast down Nimrod's tower, and caused a multitude of languages to come upon the people of earth.

Me, Nimrod, Nimrod with a lot of pride. This great hunter looking for his various prey. I wondered how he would have gone about tracking Anita. Sometimes when I go looking for birds, I'm searching out more than feathers. Coyote Hills is a good place for birding, and thinking. There's an abundance of sloughs there, and fresh-water marshes, and inlets from the bay. On the right days, it's a birder's paradise. I wasn't exactly the early birder, but didn't much care.

My binoculars identified me as a possible birder or possible pervert. The two are not necessarily mutually exclusive. Birders are a strange sort. The little-old-lady stereotype hardly applies. The average birder is a bit of a masochist. Early hours and less than ideal conditions both wet their feathers and whet their birding appetites. Difficulties make their finds that much more rewarding, war wounds to be brought out whenever there's a show of scars. And there are a lot of rituals involved with birding, rituals akin to those of other outdoor sports, especially fishing. The stories sound alike also.

When you approach someone else with binoculars, you always ask the same question: "See anything interesting today?"

And in response they usually say, "There's not that much out there, but you should have been here last week. There was everything but a dodo here."

Then you stand and make polite conversation. Sometimes they want to know just how much you know, so they mention an obscure species, or, Lord help you, spout off a Latin or Greek name. And these are the people you know can identify every bird call at a single pip, people who should have made their fortune on Name That Tweet. These are the sort who can casually turn their head and calmly tag a name on a flashing silhouette at three hundred yards, and act offended if you don't bring your binoculars to the fore with the same quickness that Marshal Matt Dillon drew his gun.

I wasn't in that league. My field checklist was pretty full, my field guide pretty scuffed, but I still had to look twice at dowitchers and sandpipers, let alone to distinguish a Semipalmated Sandpiper from a White-Rumped Sandpiper. I enjoyed being outdoors, enjoyed sighting, and identifying, and watching and learning. And so I found a comfortable promontory, looked around with my binoculars, and hoped for the unusual, scouted for the exotic, but didn't see much of either. I scanned what was there, and that was more than good enough.

Coyote Hills draws an abundance of birds. There are a number of trails and locations, all with their different feathered attractions. Today I was interested in shorebirds, and didn't bother to tramp through the willows in search of flycatchers and other small birds. The winter migration was over, so I wasn't expecting much, but one of the fascinating things about birding is that sometimes you come across the unexpected vagrant, or birds out of season. I crossed the Bay View Trail and started following the shoreline. Many of the birds that had been there in abundance a few months earlier were gone. I saw a few willets and curlews and whimbrels; most of their kind were off making little birds. There were gulls and terns, not as many ducks as I hoped for, and too many coots, which wasn't surprising.

What was surprising was the red phalarope. I stopped breathing for a moment, confirmed the sighting, then took a seat and watched the show. All birders have a few favorite species, and phalaropes happened to be one of mine. Favorite species don't have to be uncommon, and they aren't necessarily colorful. They're usually chosen for their behavior, or their personality. You're not objective about your birds, and you're ready to talk them up without much encouragement. Seeing my old friend the red phalarope gave me a little adrenaline rush.

There had been several unusual June storms, and one of them might have blown the bird in. He should have been nesting in the far north, but he was here, and I took that as an omen. Phalaropes aren't known for their striking plumage, except for females in their breeding colors. But it's not the plumage of phalaropes that attracts me; it's their work ethic. They carry a whirlpool on their small frames.

When a phalarope feeds on water it spins around like a top, stirring up whatever it can. With a wiggle of its rump, and a wag of its coverts, the phalarope is the swizzle stick of birds. They are not large, only eight to nine inches long and weighing about two ounces, but insects, larvae, crustaceans, and even little fish get swept up in their current.

My phalarope didn't disappoint me. He did his tango act. I watched as he swept forward on the water, dipped, did an enticing swirl, then swept forward again. He floated high on the water, but it wasn't pride that kept him in that position, only trapped air. Some birders describe the floating as "corking"; if that is the case, then phalaropes are of a fine vintage. My binoculars took everything in, and were only lowered reluctantly a few times to answer questions directed at me by passersby. I explained what I was looking at, but no one could understand my fascination. They could misunderstand it though, and they did.

"He's watching fallopians," one man told his wife, and she hastened him along.

I didn't correct him, didn't even add, "I've seen a few tits in my time, too." But I thought about it.

The afternoon passed. There's something Zen-like about bird watching. Through observation you meditate. And sometimes you reach a different plane. Female phalaropes do the courting, and as I watched them whirlpooling around I wondered why I hadn't heard from Ellen. I started thinking about my case and while I don't believe there's a Zen to murder investigation, I decided to act like my birds.

It was time to swirl things about.

13

I WAS AT MY office early Monday making calls, and Miss Tuntland was my first dial. She told me that a Vanessa Darling had called, and had left a number for me to call back. Miss Tuntland, ever the professional, had asked Darling the reason for her call.

"And she told me you had pressed your card on her, which got my sympathy right away," said Miss Tuntland. "I was ready to tell her that half the women in this city already have your card, but then she said something about having received it under unusual conditions. So I guessed that our Darling was probably Vincent's model, a fact she confirmed."

"Thank you," I said, "although the idea that I would bandy my business card around . . ."

"I had another call that made for an interesting party line," she said, purposely interrupting me. "There I was, along with an operator, and one Ellen Reardon. Ellen wanted to tell you how sorry she was, and wanted to get together with you as soon as possible."

"I think I'll send you two dozen doughnuts today," I said.

"Good," she said. "Giving doughnuts away is a great way to meet your neighbors. I didn't even know the handsomest man lived just two floors up from me. He said he only wanted one doughnut, but stayed around for three."

"Which left you with nine."

"You mean I didn't tell you about the stockbroker that lives right across from me?"

I think I said good-bye before hanging up, but I wouldn't have bet the farm.

Vanessa Darling was getting her beauty sleep when I woke her. To make amends I asked her out to lunch. She picked Hamburger Mary's, and we agreed to meet at one. I liked her choice. The restaurant had made it through flower children, psychedelics and gay pride. It was a place where red meat and funk came together, where the food was almost as interesting as its clients.

My next call was to Terrence Walters, and my next, and my next. My name didn't carry the cachet to get right through to him, and a cadre of buffers blocked my entree to the great man. Mr. Walters was in conference, or court, or talking with a client. The first two messages I left were within the Marquis of Queensberry Rules. The third was more on his level.

"Would you like to leave another message?" I was asked.

"Yes," I said, "tell him I'd like to discuss child molestation with him. At his convenience, of course. No need to mention prison and disbarment, just note the child molestation. Thank you very much."

There was something satisfying about doing the phalarope swirl. Stirring things up is fun as long as you don't get caught up in your own whirlpool. I was ready to do some more swirling, but stopped to do a little roost cleaning first. An office shouldn't resemble a flop house, and mine did. In one corner was an overcoat, and in the other was a newspaper. I vaguely remembered kicking the newspaper aside in the wee and staggering hours of the morning before, and stooped to pick it up. I'd had strange things dropped through my mail slot before, items I assumed were left by the stairwell squatters who frequent the neighborhood, but this offering was different from most. It wasn't all the news that's fit to print. It was a gynecological tabloid. They sell them on corners, where six or eight bits buys you cheap thrills on pulp.

I flipped through some pages which reconfirmed all my prejudices. They don't feature women in these papers, just bits and pieces of them. Breasts, vaginas, and butts, and a few more vaginas. Gynecology and misogyny, a winning combination. Not erotic, not stimulating, just locker room peep shots, and grainy ones at that. They talked about Becky's horoscope sign, and how "Becky just loves to get it on." The copy should have been written on toilet paper. I was trashing it when "Juliet" caught my eye. Under various naked pictures an oversized caption read, "Romeo, Romeo, wherefore art thou hard on, Romeo?" But it wasn't the disservice to the bard that made me cold.

Juliet was Anita.

You're not supposed to notice faces in these papers. You usually don't even see a female face clearly unless a male appendage is nearby. But I saw Anita's face. The caption said Juliet was eighteen, "and ready to take on, and in, any Montague or Capulet." It said Juliet liked partying and fast cars, "didn't know how to say 'no.' And didn't want to know how."

I noticed a few things quickly. The photographs were better than most featured in such tabloids; the newspaper was current; and if the eyes are the window to the soul, Anita didn't have one.

Her look was beyond hate, beyond any feeling. There was nothing that could be touched. She wasn't playing to the camera, wasn't sucking her stomach in and sticking her chest out, wasn't on all fours doing peek-a-boo glances. She was naked, but not exposed, baring all, but giving nothing. Anyone who looked at her face could see that, but I wondered how many people would notice her face. In her lifetime, I wondered how many people had.

The hollow in my stomach didn't fill on my way to Tiburon. It wasn't relieved by the view, and the cozy little stores. I walked into Kevin Bateson's studio, and the blonde receptionist didn't try to say a halting word. Not even a peep. There was that kind of look on my face.

Bateson was in back. He was by himself. He made the mistake of saying, "Hey," and for that I pushed him out of the way. Hard. I walked into his office, and opened the appropriate filing cabinet. There were two Anita Walters folders. I lifted them both. One I had seen. The other was the birthday-suit variety.

I scrutinized the photos one by one. Bateson had found a seat by that time, one near the door. He didn't want to take any chances, and his was a wise decision. I finished looking at the pictures, then opened up Juliet's sexpaper pictorial for Bateson to see.

"Look familiar?"

Bateson nodded.

"Tell me about it."

Bateson didn't answer right away. "You have five seconds to say something. Silence gets you the police."

"I've had those pictures for a while," he said at about the one-second mark. He was a little sullen, and a little frightened. "They were just sitting here. I sold them to the paper around two months ago."

"Why?"

"Money."

"How much were you paid for the pictures?"

"Three hundred dollars."

"Three hundred dollars? That was your incentive?"

He nodded. I picked up his phone and started dialing.

"Who are you calling?" he asked.

"The police," I said. "They'll want to know why a successful photographer is selling nude photos of a missing woman for about what it must have cost him to do the shoot."

His answers were coming a little more quickly now, and with a bit more truth. "It wasn't for the money, not totally.

"I thought she might see the pictures, might get mad enough to come out from wherever she was and see me. It was a way I thought I could reach her."

"When did you take the pictures?"

"Early December."

"Had she posed nude for you before?"

"No."

"Tell me about that session."

Bateson's reluctance appeared again. "Maybe I should talk with an attorney."

"Fine. Tell him to meet us at the police station."

He clenched his hands. "It's not that I really did anything wrong," he said. "It's not that way at all."

I didn't say anything.

"It was here. I was working late. I didn't know she would be coming over. I never did."

"Do you know sign language?"

"No."

"Then how'd you talk with her?"

"She could always make her wishes known. Usually she didn't need a pencil and paper. She made you understand."

"The last time we talked you said you had never been intimate with her."

"That's right."

"And I suppose you're going to tell me these are just some artistic nude shots."

"No."

"So why'd she take her clothes off?"

He hesitated. "I asked her to."

I looked at him. "Pretend I can't talk," I said. "If Anita was giving you my look, what would she be saying?"

"That I'm lying."

I nodded. "Very good. And what about this look?"

"Tell the real story."

"You've convinced me you're perceptive," I said, "now make me a little more of a believer."

He took a breath, and when he exhaled decided to chance the truth. "It was late afternoon. Cleo, my receptionist, had left, but the place wasn't locked up. Anita just appeared. I wasn't expecting her, hadn't seen her for three or four weeks, but there she was. Anita was like that. Showed up when you didn't expect her. I was glad to see her, she knew that, but I told her I had to finish up what I was doing. I gave her a magazine, but Anita's never been very good at waiting. She came over to see what I was doing, leaned on me and looked at some pictures I was developing.

"Some of the shots were risqué. I had been commissioned to do a lingerie line, and Anita found that amusing. She picked up a proof sheet and started prancing around. She practiced the poses of the models, parodied the parodies. At first I laughed, but she became more and more of a pest. Then she turned into a tease. She unbuttoned some blouse buttons, and hiked up her skirt, mimicked some of the racier lingerie."

"But she didn't take her clothes off?"

"No. Just teased. And that was bad enough. It was a sore spot."

"Why?"

"The fight we had—the one that broke us up—it was too close to that. While she was still at Greenmont I shot some pictures of her in a bikini. I tried to get close to her, and she wouldn't let me."

"You came on to her, and she rejected your advances."

"Yeah."

"She stopped your personal and professional relationship because of that?"

"Yeah."

"Read my look again."

Bateson didn't even bother to look. He pouted, then finally answered. "You're right. It wasn't only my pass. It was what I said. She read my lips too well. I didn't like being pushed away by a girl I desired. Maybe loved even. But that's not what I told her. I told her she wasn't that hot anyway, and that Kevin Bateson could have a dozen of her on any day. I told her she was cold, and probably frigid, and not worthy of me. I said a lot of other things, none very smart, and I stung her pride. You don't do that to Anita."

"You apologized?"

"A hundred times. It didn't do any good. She remembered the hurting words, not the healing ones."

"So what magic words did you use to get her clothes off?"

He got the cornered look on his face again. Pretty boys like Bateson usually had things go their way. He had a smooth patter, good looks, a job where his nails never got dirty, and his hair stayed blow-dry fine. He wasn't deep, wasn't happy to be reminded that there had been a yesterday, and that he might have acted in a manner that went against the GQ style.

"She became more of a brat," he said. "She wouldn't give the proof sheet back ..."

"What did you do?"

"I-I got physical with her because she wouldn't give ..."

"What did you do?"

"I grabbed her ..."

"Did you hit her?"

"'A few times, but ..."

"How many times?"

"Two or three ..."

"Five or six?"

"Maybe."

"And then what?"

"I said I had been nice to her for too long."

"She couldn't hear. How did she know what you were saying?"

"I held her head. I made her read my lips."

"Did you slap her?"

He still avoided my eyes. I was tempted to hold his head like he had Anita's. "I might have," he said.

"And then what?"

"She took off her clothes."

"On your suggestion only, I'm sure."

"I knew she'd done it for a couple of artists. I didn't think it was any big deal. What's the difference between art and photography?"

"Did she take her clothes off willingly?"

"She was sort of in a daze."

"You knocked her silly, didn't you?"

He didn't answer.

"Did you strip her?"

"I ripped off a button or two. Then she started to undress herself."

"Did she look at you?"

"No."

"Was she bleeding?"

"A little from the mouth."

"Of course, you cleaned that up for the pictures."

I don't think he heard the sarcasm. "Yeah. And then I took her to the set."

"Roughly?"

"I was still mad. Maybe a push or two."

I looked at her naked pictures in the sexpaper, and I looked at Bateson. "What happened when you took these?"

"Nothing."

"Nothing?"

"She was sort of out of it."

"How out of it?"

"It was like I wasn't there."

I sorted out the negatives from Bateson's file, then held them up to the light. Something didn't look right in them, not that I expected anything right could have come out of that session. Anita had been attacked and beaten, then set in front of a camera. Her eyes were as dead as they should have been, and her body as lifeless. But her hands bothered me. They were held up and out, like a tired beggar who knows alms won't be forthcoming, but still instinctively reaches out a claw to a passerby. I kept looking at the negatives. My first impression was wrong. It wasn't that she looked like a supplicant. Not exactly. There was a better description, but one I kept falling short of making. I mulled over the shots for another minute, but the word, the answer, wasn't there.

"Tell me about these shots," I said, throwing the negatives at Bateson.

He looked at them, smoothed an out of place hair. "They were early in the shoot," he said. "She kept moving her hands."

"I thought you said she was out of it."

"She was."

"So how'd you get her hands down? How'd you get her to stop."

"With persuasion."

"You hit her?"

"Just her hands mostly."

"What a gentleman."

"I was a jerk. I know. And when I cooled down I apologized for everything. God, I apologized."

"And what happened?"

"Nothing at first. Then it was like Anita woke up. She slapped me, hard, and I took it. I wish she had slapped me a few more times, but she didn't. She just looked at me with a lot of hate, and then she left."

"And you haven't seen her since?"

"Right."

I gathered up Anita's portfolio. Bateson knew better than to object, but he did ask, "What are you going to do with those?"

Nastiness wasn't far from my tongue. But it wasn't going to change Kevin Bateson. I threw him the gynecological paper. His hands were slow, and it hit him in his face. Anita's pictorial, Juliet's, separated around the room. I remembered a line from that play, and I felt right in saying it.

"She speaks, yet she says nothing."

Bateson didn't ask for a translation, and I didn't give him one.

Vanessa Darling was waiting in front of the restaurant. She was wearing a colored serape, and her reddish hair was pulled under a sailor's cap. I almost walked by her before she caught my attention.

I used one of the oldest lines in burlesque, which had thankfully died with vaudeville: "I almost didn't recognize you with your clothes on."

Vanessa had the good sense to groan.

The restaurant was crowded. We were seated next to the bus station, so we carried on most of our conversation over water glasses being filled. Since the place was also noisy, we found ourselves huddled together. It wasn't sensual, just necessary. Early in our conversation Vanessa said that she was "living with her lover—Suzanne." She didn't say it to shock me, or warn me away, but just as an aside on her life.

"My old lady's an artist too," she said. "I model for her, but don't get paid."

"And probably don't get smeared with paint."

Vanessa had been a model for a few years. She told me about some of the artists she had worked for, and admitted she had "a thing" for artists. Most of her lovers had been men, and most had been poor artists. I let her ramble for a while, and then I told her about my case. She had heard of Anita, but had never met her, and couldn't add anything about her life that I didn't already know.

"So tell me about the life of an art model, then," I said.

"It's mostly a bitch," said Vanessa. "The pay's shitty, and you've always got to deal with artistic temperament. That's not a made-up phrase."

"Like Vincent?" I asked.

"You saw him in one of his intense moments."

"Is that what you call it?"

"Sometimes he needs to do things like that for inspiration."

"Is that what he says?"

"He says it facilitates his vision, or something like that."

"You looked scared."

"I was a little. He's strong, and his hands are rough. It hurt when he rubbed the paint on me."

"Has he hurt you before? Scared you?"

"I wouldn't call it scared."

"What would you call it?"

"Sometimes he puts me off balance."

"How often?"

"Every few weeks."

"And what does he do?"

"He likes different poses, sometimes difficult ones. And he's so intense. He'll yell at you if you can't hold it."

"What else?"

"I've heard some of his other models complain."

"And what do they say?"

"They don't like the way he talks sometimes."

"What do you mean?"

"He doesn't do it with me, just some of the girls."

"And what's that?"

"It's—well, it's like he fantasizes out loud. Fantasizes about weird things."

"Can you give me an example?"

"Well, one girl I know, Tricia, said she was doing a painting with him once, I think it was called 'Salem Witch Trial,' or something like that. And he had all the Puritans in black and wearing caps, and made them look like the witches and warlocks, while he had the real witch, or what was supposed to be the witch, looking normal. So he started talking about witches, and asked Tricia what she would do if she was a witch. Then he started getting weird. He asked Tricia if she'd make love while riding her broomstick, and asked her how she'd enchant her lovers, and what she'd do with them. Then he started saying he knew what kind of spells she'd cast, and they were bizarre things. And she could see he was getting excited—physically, I mean. He was painting furiously, and all the while he turned to her and said stuff like, 'Then you'd make the minister run naked through the pumpkin patch, make him act like he was in rut, wouldn't you?' Tricia said she was so scared she agreed to whatever he said."

"Why does anyone work for Vincent?"

"He pays well. And he's good. It's sort of a status thing for models, who you're working for. Everybody wants their piece of immortality."

"And that's worth freezing in an unheated loft? Or getting tetanus from the filth on the floor? Haven't any of the models ever complained about the mess in that place?"

"Vincent doesn't believe in waste. He likes his oddments. That's what he calls them. He makes sculptures and decorative pieces from absolute junk, things just lying around. He's got a thing against throwing stuff away. He's sort of obsessed about getting use out of everything, even discards."

"How long have you been working for him?"

"On and off for a year and a half."

"Do you know any of Vincent's lovers?"

"Yeah. A few of his models, but they didn't make any

big thing about it, and neither did Vincent. And then of
course there's Goldilocks."

"You know Goldilocks?"

"Yeah. Sometimes I think she makes Vincent seem normal."

"Do you think Vincent and Anita were lovers?"

"No one ever said anything. I kinda doubt it. I remember someone said Anita was a tight ass."

"Who said that?"

"I don't remember."

We talked for about a half hour longer than our food
lasted, two figures huddling to hear, and maybe for a little
warmth. I heard Vanessa's opinions on life. They weren't
jaded, which was refreshing. She was a pretty woman, not
overly intelligent, but without guile. I liked her openness,
her bounce. She lived in a world where weird was normal.
Maybe we all did. But it didn't faze her.

"Do you paint?" she finally asked me.

"Only in water," I said.

"I like watercolors," she said.

"I do, too."

"Hey, if you hear of anyone who needs a model . . ."

"I'll tell them they couldn't do any better."

"And thanks for lunch. It was a trip."

We passed smiles, and then separated. I watched the
wind tug at her serape, watched her hold firmly to her cap.

It was a trip, she had said. A trip where, I wondered.

14

WHEN I CHECKED IN with Miss Tuntland, I learned that Terrence Walters had not returned my call. It didn't surprise me. My message had been premature, not to mention stupid. I was glad for two things: my message hadn't been specific, and I had already cashed Tammy Walters's check. Not too many employers like to be accused of child molestation, especially without tangible evidence. Terrence Walters might even give an aggrieved squawk to the Department of Consumer Affairs. Their watchdogs overlooked the Collection and Investigative Services, and had the right to take away an investigator's license for a "crime of moral turpitude."

But moral turpitude wasn't the major crime in question. It was murder. Even if my theory of child molestation fit, it wasn't likely to help with the case I was working on. Anita's possible abuse was just another windmill unless I believed her father had killed her. It wasn't a theory I ruled out, but filicide didn't seem Terrence Walters's style. If Anita had threatened to expose his past sins, he probably would have found a way to discredit her, something far short of murder. And if he had killed Anita, I didn't think he would have allowed his wife to hire a private investigator. Terrence Walters was too much of a thinker for that. He would have found a safer way to show his Piedmont neighbors his filial concern.

I asked Miss Tuntland about my other calls. A long list

of delayed professional calls were adding up. I kept putting off making those calls, knowing that they would bring on conferences and new deadlines. But there was one call that wasn't professional. Ellen Reardon and the operator had called again.

I felt a little better for the news. The day wasn't much more than halfway over, but I was tired already, almost ready to call Ellen and be pampered. I attended to business first though, and used my change to call Tammy Walters. Her vibrant voice didn't change too noticeably after I identified myself. I acted like I was too busy to talk, and quickly made my request to visit with her the next day. She agreed to my coming over the following day at three, and even said she looked forward to it. Politeness often gets in the way of truth.

My next call was to Ellen and the operator. It was good hearing both of them. I let myself be talked into a dinner at seven at Ellen's place. Neither the operator nor Ellen had to coax very much.

I didn't have any more change, but I did have four hours. I debated options, and decided on a long shot. Anita Walters's last reported destination was the New Year's celebration in North Beach. I wondered whether she ever made it. The authorities hadn't made a determination one way or the other, had let that, and Anita, fall through the cracks.

I wasn't a stranger to the festivities. Every year the crowds grew so heavy that the police closed off Broadway and Columbus. It was the bedlam of the City trying to throw off its cares. People with horns and costumes and masks marched up and down the streets. Street performers abounded, and made for great spectator sport. The police almost made it a parade, the mounted police, the cavalry, marching up and down with their horses, a procession of order on a night of madness. If Anita had gone out that night, and her mother said she never missed the New

Year's festivities, she would have been just one of many celebrants.

Which made me wonder if anyone had seen her.

Among all the glitter, all the get-ups, all the milling, I wondered if my needle had somehow stood out in the hay. I had her picture, the clothed one, and I went to North Beach with it. The unclothed photo would have drawn more interest, especially in North Beach, but I doubt if it would have helped the case more than the clothed one. I approached merchants and residents, and tried to tell my story in the hopes that it would buy thirty seconds of thought, but thinking is a hard sell these days. A police badge probably would have held more weight than my business card, but maybe not. Foolishness is foolishness. New Year's was six months past, and not a few people reminded me of that. No one remembered seeing Anita on the night of December thirty-first. I told them she was deaf, in the hopes her disability might have stood out, and might jar their memories, but it didn't.

I heard "sorry's," and "no's." A number of men appreciated Anita's beauty, and I wished I had a dollar for every one that said, "Never saw her, don't know her, but wish I did." But those were the good answers compared to the mummer's reception I too often faced. Every third or fourth person didn't want to be involved. I couldn't get them to look at the picture—they just walked by me. It was hard for me to accept their indifference.

A street person watched me get the brushoff, watched as someone paused the barest moment to hear me out before continuing on as if I weren't there. He observed me, so I observed him. He was aged, but ageless, and had the look of a survivor. My discomfiture at not getting a response appeared to amuse him. To survive, he knew how to maintain his equanimity with rejection. He lived daily with refusal, with people who made a point of not noticing him. He was reclined next to a building in what could charitably be called a comfortable position. His legs, housed in dirty dungarees, blocked a good part of the sidewalk, but people managed to skirt by the obstacle without really seeing. A full brown bag also rested horizontally on the sidewalk. The contents of the bag had loosened his tongue. He was the first person to solicit my inquiry.

"Whatcha looking for?"

I approached him without much hope.

"Missing girl," I said. "Been missing since December thirty-first. She might have been part of the New Year's street celebration around here."

"Lemme see."

He waved his hands, and I was reluctant to put a clean picture into fingers that were waving flags of nicotine and grime. But I got by that prejudice. There were other pictures, and this was a man who wanted to help. He didn't have anything, but he still wanted to help.

He squinted, the red rims of his eyes closing into what looked like an opened scab. He held the picture for a long time. I wondered what kind of memories it brought back. He gave back the picture reluctantly, like he would a bottle with a swallow left.

"Nope," he said. "Never saw her."

I thanked him, and was ready go pass by, when the honk of another wild goose sounded in my head. Winter's law is that when you pursue futility, you may as well pursue it fully.

"How's your bottle doing?" I asked.

The man was immediately suspicious, good will at an end. "Empty," he said.

I waved a ten. "This will fill it then some if you do me a favor."

"What?"

"Talk to the street people around here. Get them to come talk with me. Tell them a man's asking questions. Tell them I'll take everybody for coffee and doughnuts."

"Give me the money and I'll do it."

I committed a federal crime by ripping the ten in half. He got both of Hamilton's eyes, but only half the bill.

"I'll be back in a few minutes," he said. He picked up his bottle, threw it in his coat, and walked away more quickly than I would have guessed possible. I listened to his empty bottle slosh.

The longer I waited, the more stupid I felt. I had worked with the homeless on previous cases, and the results were rarely satisfactory. Most indigents have bad memories. They are usually poor because they have minimal or non-existent reading or writing skills. Reading and writing reinforces memory. The written word allows reference points that most people secure their anchors to while life swirls around. Street people don't have those anchors. For them, distinguishing yesterday from a year ago is virtually impossible.

But still I stood. There was a dinner waiting for me, but I knew it wouldn't settle as well without one last throw of the dice. Fifteen minutes passed, then twenty, then half an hour. If Hamilton hadn't already been decapitated, I would have accepted the fact that I was stood up, and even knowing that, I was almost ready to give up my vigil. Then they appeared, as rag-a-tag an assemblage as the City could muster. Vincent might have done justice to the painting.

There were seven of them, and from the looks on the faces of observers, the bubonic plague might have been on the move again. I approached them, while everyone else made a point of walking away.

"See," said my messenger, "I told you he'd be here."

He waved his hand at me, ready for a paper bonding, but I pretended ignorance, and didn't have to pretend suspicion. The group massed around me.

"I have some questions I'd like to ask you," I said.

"Where's the wine?" someone asked.

I looked at the messenger, who looked away and mumbled something. "I only promised coffee and doughnuts," I said, an announcement that was met with general disgust. "But," I added, "seeing it's getting a little nippy, how about I get a couple bottles of brandy to add to our coffee?" This announcement was better received.

Finding the brandy was easier than getting the coffee. I led my troop to the coffee house, and was met at the door by the manager.

"No way," he said.

I could have argued the point, could have pointed out that we were paying customers, but in his own way he was right. The group of us probably would have curdled the café au lait of all his patrons. And I wasn't too keen on being in an enclosed space with my newfound friends, either.

"Seven coffees to go," I said, "and fourteen pastries."

I've never had such prompt service. If you're ever in a rush, just bring along a bunch of the homeless. I followed the group to a nearby alleyway, and there made generous with the brandy. A few managed to spill most of their coffee before I began my pour.

They finished their pastries and coffee quickly, hungry dogs at a plate, and assembled their cups to finish off the bottles. The preliminaries taken care of, they were more disposed toward talk. I passed around Anita's picture, and asked everyone to look at it carefully. I told them about her deafness, and asked them to think back to New Year's. The date was lucky for me. New Year's is usually the major holiday for the homeless. Drinks are easier to cadge, and people are more ready to produce a quarter. Everybody comes to their turf to get drunk, and usually an extra bottle or two finds its way to the hands of the regulars.

Most of them remembered New Year's. They remembered getting a better bottle of booze than usual, remembered getting more free drinks. But they didn't remember Anita, or didn't think they did.

"Saw some pretty girls that night," said one, "all dressed up, real pretty. But don't remember that one."

They all agreed to that refrain. Everyone except the one they called Shorty, a man who lived down to his name. "I seen her," he said, but even he didn't sound like he believed himself.

"I think I seen her," he said, and there were a few coughs, and a few laughs.

In each strata of society there is a pecking order. The terms comes from hens in the hen house. They all know who they can peck, and who can peck them. The alpha hen can peck everyone, and not get pecked by any. Then there is the poor omega hen, the hen that everyone pecks with impunity, knowing they won't get pecked back. Even among the so-called riff raff there is a hierarchy, and Shorty was definitely at the bottom rung. I felt sorry for him, and tried to act like I believed him, even if I didn't.

"What do you remember?" I asked.

"The girl," he said.

A few derisive remarks were mouthed, a few people said I was stupid to even be listening.

"What was she wearing?"

"A pretty dress."

There were a few more laughs.

"Do you remember the color?"

"No."

"Was she with anyone?"

"I don't know."

Just about everyone was laughing now.

"Why'd you notice her? Was she using sign language? Doing something out of the ordinary?"

"I don't know."

Shorty didn't like the laughter. He had heard too much in his time. His peers had dropped him below the dog droppings. He kicked his foot around the ground, shuffling some garbage from an overflowing dumpster. Then his foot stopped moving, and his head raised again.

"Her ear," he said triumphantly.

"You noticed her hearing aid?"

"No. Her ear. It was all bandaged. I heard some people ask her about it, but she didn't say nothing."

"Her ear was bandaged?"

Shorty nodded. He looked proud, looked around to everyone else. They were quiet now, even a bit surprised. I decided not to put any doubt on my face, decided to let Shorty have a moment of glory. I solemnly thanked everyone, and Shorty in particular. They disbanded one by one, scuttling out and away. I was left with my messenger. I handed him the remaining half of the bill. He took it without thanks, and followed the path of his brethren.

Ellen met me at her door. She looked like she was ready to hug me, but I stopped her with a raised hand. Who said I didn't know sign language?

"I definitely need a shower," I said. "I need one so much I wouldn't want to hug anyone who hugged me."

That made her laugh. She led me to the shower, showed me where the towels were, then lingered around the bathroom. She didn't pretend to have something else to do, just smiled and watched me strip, and looked ready to apply the soap at the least encouragement.

I always take short showers. I don't like to waste the water or the time. But I indulged myself a little longer than usual, soaked away a day of Kevin Bateson, and Vanessa Darlin, and Shorty. The shower pulsed and I purred. When I finished, I felt human again.

Ellen was waiting with a towel. "Is it safe to hug you now?" she asked. I shook some water at her, and she rubbed me down. Then she led me to her bedroom.

"It's definitely all right to hug me now," I said.

We hugged for a long time, and then she made me feel

more than human, which is a good feeling indeed. Sometime that night we remembered dinner. It had been left to warm for a few hours, but didn't suffer for the delay. Ellen had made a chicken Florentine. The dish was new to me, but I fell in love with it. We got around to our before dinner drinks after dinner.

"We never go about things in the usual way," I said.

"Are you complaining?"

"No."

We talked about nothing and everything. I heard about her parents and her brother. Learned she liked dogs, but that her lease forbade her having one. She told me about getting a new commission for a quilt, and I found myself telling her some things, also. I told her about my work, and even about my life before investigation. I knew better than to mention the current case. Ellen was still jealous of Anita. She would be jealous until she went to her grave, and jealous even if Anita was already in hers.

We made love again. It was like the wine we had been drinking, gentle, smooth, and warming. When we finished, we were both ready for sleep.

"Don't leave this time without kissing me," she said.

"I won't," I said, "I promise."

"Sweet dreams."

"Sweet dreams."

But my dreams weren't so sweet. I awoke around four, shouting, I think, Anita's name. She wouldn't let me go during the day, and now she controlled my nights. It was the same dream as before, the same nightmare.

Ellen's back was turned to me. I hadn't awakened her. I took a few deep breaths, thought about my dream, and remembered the frustration of not being able to communicate with Anita.

"It's only a dream," I told myself, but it was a dream that kept me up thinking. The case was there whether my eyes were open or closed. The images didn't stop, the pictures of naked Anita, Anita of the glazed eyes and distorted hands. And there were Shorty's words I kept hearing: "Her ear. It was all bandaged."

I got up with the sun and dressed. I kissed Ellen and she stirred. "It's too early," she whispered.

"Yes," I whispered back.

My lips reassured her again. She read them like lips should be read.

15

I TOOK THE BAY Bridge back into the City. San Franciscans are chauvinistic about their home, worse than Parisians or New Yorkers. Mencken wrote about visiting San Francisco, and explained in a sentence what the City is all about: "What fetched me instantly was the subtle but unmistakable sense of escape from the United States." To a resident of Baghdad by the Bay, there's San Francisco, and then there's a world out there. In that order. And never the twain should meet.

I gave short shrift to my morning ritual of the *Chronicle* and Miss Tuntland. For a while I looked at the photos of the nude but lifeless Anita. There wasn't anything prurient in my interest, or at least not much. The pictures bothered me even if I didn't know why. Ten minutes produced no revelations, and I finally put them aside.

A business suit was in order for the day, a conservative business suit with undertaker appeal. I made a few calls, then picked out some appropriate business cards. A car legitimates some people. They live to hand out their two-by-three-and-one-halfs, and I always accept their offering.

Today I was Peter Brooks, CPA. I worked for No More Tears Accounting. I didn't remember Mr. Brooks, but if he thought up the firm's name, maybe it was a memory I suppressed.

I drove over to the Berkeley Hills and scouted out the hospitals nearest to the Gorilla Project. The proximity winner wasn't a hospital, but a quick-care medical center, the kind that dealt with stitches, sore throats, and less advanced cases of syphilis. I took myself and my gray suit to the desk, and asked whom I might talk to about an accounting question. I was directed to Miss Phelps and an office in the back.

Miss Phelps was a thirtyish veteran of many invoice questions. I presented my card and said good-bye to Peter Brooks. There were four other CPA's in my wallet behind him.

"Good morning," I said, "I'm Peter Brooks. I work for Dr. Harrison and the Gorilla Project, and he asked me to look into something for him."

Miss Phelps was all patient boredom.

"We've been getting invoices from your establishment for a patient admitted on December thirty-first. Our records show we paid that bill."

Miss Phelps raised one eyebrow. "That's unusual," she said. "We usually require payment on the premises. Our policy is to not even bill for insurance. We put that responsibility on the individual who's being treated."

I titled my head in mock surprise, and added a little eye movement which was supposed to represent accounting umbrage. "Then I don't understand . . ." I said.

"No. Dr. Harrison just told me about them over the phone. And as I was driving by . . ."

"Why don't we look it up then?"

"I'd appreciate that."

"Do you know the name of the patient?"

"Yes. Anita Walters."

"And that was on December thirty-first?"

"Yes."

The woman entered some information on her computer. She frowned, which made me frown, and then punched a few more keys.

"I don't understand this," she said.

I readied myself for another explanation.

"This shows that the bill was paid in full on December thirty-first."

Miss Phelps provided me with a computer printout. Without a medical degree I translated the treatment: 36 stitches had been needed to treat Anita Walters's lacerated external left ear. She had been admitted at five o'clock. Payment by check had been made at seven-thirty by a Dr. William Henry Harrison.

There was a lot to think about on my way to the Gorilla Project. I made one stop, and one call, before I pulled the Olds up to the gate. I didn't feel any better for my call. It made me suspect, just a little more, that Dr. Harrison was a murderer.

I didn't want to think so. I wanted to be wrong. Dr. Harrison was the Dr. Doolittle of the media. He walked with his animals, and more amazingly, he talked with the animals. His obvious love for his furry charges was well reported. How far his devotion had taken him was what I wondered.

I drove up the graveled road and parked next to the ranch house. When I had asked Joseph what happened to Anita, he had stared out to the bamboo field. That's where I walked. The bamboo shoots were up to my waist. I wondered about their fertilizer, and about a lot of things as I stood and looked around.

Company came in less than five minutes. It was the same young man who had admonished me for interfering with Joseph's lessons the week before. He had the same complaint this time. He said that Joseph was on his tire looking at me, and that I had to go inside the house if he was to continue with his lessons. I ignored him for a few seconds, and took that time to wave to Joseph. I could see the window, but not him. It was too dark. But I could feel his presence.

The young man was getting very exasperated. I finally

turned to him. "I'm sorry," I said, "but I won't be leaving this field until Dr. Harrison comes out to talk with me."

The young man looked at me as if I were crazy—the young man who taught gorillas their A-B-C's.

"Tell Dr. Harrison that Stuart Winter, and Anita Walters, are waiting for him."

The message brought Harrison out to the bamboo field. He came out too quickly, and too ready to bluster. His face was flushed and his index finger was already pointing. I interrupted his threats before they began.

"Is Anita Walters buried in this field?"

The question silenced him, and changed his flush to a pallor.

"I just called a nursery," I said. "I asked them if bamboo should be planted in January. They advised against it. Strongly advised."

Harrison's voice was whispery. "That hardly qualifies . . ."

"The last time I was here I asked Joseph what happened to Anita. I think he's the only person who hasn't lied to me on this case, who hasn't guised the truth in a more acceptable form. And when I asked him what happened to Anita, he just looked out here. I think he told me something. Did you bury her here?"

Dr. Harrison's fingers were trembling. "No, she's not buried here."

"Then what was Joseph telling me?"

Harrison didn't answer right away. "I forgot about Joseph," he said. "That explains why he was upset for so long. He probably still is."

"He's got company. What happened on December thirty-first, Dr. Harrison?"

He chose to be evasive. "I'd rather not talk about it."

I added some straw to his bending back. "I think you had better, Dr. Harrison. If you don't, I'll have to go to the media, the media that dotes on you. And I will tell them you've lied, and covered up, and possibly murdered. And I will tell them that your great apes are a danger to their trainers, and possibly the community."

The last sentence, the last straw, hurt the most. His bent shoulders started heaving, dry sobs moving them. "No, you mustn't."

"I'll show them Anita's doctor bill, the one where she required thirty-six stitches. I'll tell them that Joseph inflicted the wound, and that you covered it up. I'll get Anita's picture splashed on the front page of every newspaper, and with her face staring out of every news broadcast, my investigation might be helped. That is, if Anita's not buried in this field."

"She's not," he said again.

"I'd prefer not going to the media, Dr. Harrison. I'd prefer your telling me what happened on December thirty-first. Then I'll leave your world as intact as I can."

Dr. Harrison took a few deep breaths. There was a lot of will in the man, enough to steel himself quickly for some unpleasant admissions. But he was the parent first, the forgiving parent. Children don't commit sins. Peccadillos maybe, but never outright sins. "It wasn't really Joseph's fault," he said, "wasn't really at all."

And with that dispensation he continued. "It was at the end of their session. There was no one else there. Anita must have been looking away, must have been daydreaming.

"My guess is he grabbed at her, just like children do. It would only have been a game to him. But he's so strong. He probably pulled her head against the cage—that would explain her contusions—and then grabbed her ear. She must have struggled, and that was her mistake. You don't try to wrench something from a gorilla. That makes them hold on all the harder. But Anita was panicked, I'm sure of that. She pulled and he tugged, and her hear was half ripped from her head."

"You didn't see any of this?"

"No."

"You heard her screaming?"

"No. I don't think she screamed. I think I would have heard that. I was outside, putting the dog in his pen, but I never heard anything. I saw her stagger from the bungalow. She was bleeding profusely."

"What did you do?"

"I tried to stop the bleeding. I tried to calm her down. She was in shock."

"What was she saying? Signing?"

"As I said, she was in shock. She really didn't know what she was signing."

"And what didn't she know she was signing?"

"She signed, 'No, no. Stop it. No more.' Something like that. She thought I was her father. She was very dazed, very confused."

"What did you do with her?"

"I led her to the front of the house and sat her down. I ran into the house and got some towels. There was so much blood."

"And what did she sign during that time?"

"Nothing at first. She was quiet while I tended to her. She only started signing when I said we'd have to take her to the hospital."

"What did she sign?"

Harrison didn't speak. He didn't want to remember. Only one thing could have struck him that deeply.

"She threatened Joseph, didn't she?"

Harrison nodded. "I didn't expect that. She said Joseph attacked her. She said he should be destroyed. She said she would sue the project."

"And what did you do?'

"I asked her what happened, and then tried to explain, to show her that Joseph didn't really attack her, that he was just playing. She should have known that, but she turned . . ."

"Vicious?"

"Yes. Vicious. She took the towel from her ear and shook it at me. Blood splashed all over. She signed she wasn't going to be my victim, wasn't going to be anybody's victim."

"What did you do?"

"I kept telling her to calm down, that we had to get her treated. Finally, she stopped her signing. She let me lead her to the truck."

"Did you talk on your drive to the hospital?"

"No. I started to, but I couldn't meet her eyes. There was too much anger there."

The bell of truth sounded a little off. "Or maybe you were too guilty to look at her," I said. "Maybe you had already thought up the lie you were going to tell at the hospital, and knew Anita would be able to read it."

"No." And then two seconds later, "Maybe."

"So you filled out the forms at the desk, and did all the talking with the nurses and the doctor."

"Yes."

"And you told them Anita fell, and struck her ear against a metal bar."

"Yes."

"Did Anita know you were lying?"

"I don't know. I tried to avert my mouth from her when I told the story at the center."

"But she might have seen you lie?"

"Yes."

"So she loved an ape that hurt her, maimed her even. And then you lied, a man she probably respected more than any other. And what did your lie do? It put her in the position of once more having to defend herself."

Harrison didn't like my version. "But you can see," he said, "it wasn't Joseph's fault. He can't defend himself, so

I did. I tried to avoid a circus. My research, my gorillas, were never meant for the Ringling Brothers. Gorillas are sensitive, very sensitive."

I was glad his self-righteous steam didn't take him too far. His only sin was loving his children too much. "What else did you say to Anita that night?"

"I tried to talk with her on the ride back. But she wouldn't acknowledge my signs."

"What were you signing?"

"How sorry I was. How Joseph's actions weren't malicious. How I'd make it up to her."

"And she didn't sign anything back?"

"No."

"What happened when you returned?"

"I asked her to come in the house, but she wouldn't. She just stood next to the truck in the driveway."

"That would be out of Joseph's line of vision, wouldn't it?"

"Yes."

"And what did you do then?"

"I told her she should stay for the night. And when she didn't respond to that, I offered to get her a robe, said that would be much better than her bloody clothes. But she still didn't respond, and still wouldn't follow me, so I went inside and got her the robe."

"And she just stayed outside in the cold?"

"Yes."

"What happened after you brought her the robe?"

"I asked her in again, but she ignored me. So then I signed to her that I was going inside to make her some tea. When I came out with the tea I saw she had changed into the robe. Her bloody clothes were on the ground. I told her I'd have them dry-cleaned, and if the blood didn't come out I'd have them replaced. And then she finally signed back."

He said her words slowly, even unconsciously signed

them while he spoke. They were words that had haunted him. "She said she didn't want the clothes back. She said the only replacement she wanted for them was a gorilla coat."

"And what did you do?"

"You mean, did I murder her? Is that your question, Mr. Winter?"

"Yes. That's my question."

"I did not. I considered somehow stopping her, but didn't know how. It was later that night when I thought about murder, one of those fleeting visions, the kind you think about but dismiss in the same second. But in that second, I wondered whether I could do it."

"And could you?"

"To protect Joseph and Bathsheba I could. Yes."

"But you didn't murder. What did you do?"

"I decided to hide the accident. I turned on all the outside lights. I took all of her bloody clothes, and mine, and buried them. Then I went into Joseph's bungalow and scoured the floor. I didn't want any trace of the blood. I did the same with the truck."

"Did you talk with Joseph?"

"No. I was too busy. But tonight I will talk with him. He knows about death. He saw us bury a cat once, and asked a lot of questions. He saw his mother die while he clung to her. With all that blood and activity, Joseph must have thought he killed Anita."

"Why the bamboo?"

"I'd been talking about planting it for some time. I decided if anyone asked about the digging out back I would say it was in preparation for the bamboo. I planted seeds a few days later and it's actually done quite well. We didn't have any frost this year."

"But if Anita hadn't disappeared, if she had gone to the authorities and tried to have Joseph taken from you, would you have persisted in your lies?"

Harrison didn't like himself at that moment. "Probably," he said. "Yes."

I let his own indictment hang in the air for a few seconds. "When did she leave?" I asked.

"It must have been about eight o'clock."

"And she just drove off wearing your robe?"

"No. She changed. Most of the workers here keep a spare set of clothes."

"She went to a New Year's celebration," I said. "Don't you find it strange that a woman who has just experienced a severe laceration to her ear would have the moxie to go out that same night?" •

"When Anita makes up her mind," he said, "I've found her to be a very determined woman."

"That being the case," I said, "You must have been very concerned about her threats."

Harrison averted his eyes and said nothing.

"How did you explain Anita's absence to others at the Project?"

"I described her accident—my version of it. I said she wouldn't be back for some time. People forget."

"But gorillas don't."

"Yes, that's right."

Harrison and I talked for five minutes longer. I think he became as happy as humanly possible—in a human presence possible that is—when I told him his secret probably wouldn't have to go beyond me and Joseph. I asked him about Anita's disappearance, but he had no idea what could have happened to her. For the sake of his charges, I had the feeling he hoped I wouldn't find her soon.

I asked him one last question. I positioned my hands and asked him to translate my signing. He tried to explain about Ameslan, and how it could be interpreted differently, and how signs were often used in the context of others, but I shushed his hedging. I asked him what I was saying.

And he told me.

I wasn't surprised, just a little more angry.

16

It HAD BEEN a long time between invitations to Piedmont. Once upon a time I had visited regularly. Piedmont hadn't changed, but I had. The mansions were still there, and the people behind the mansions—people who didn't pop their p's or forget to say please. The letter P kept surfacing in my mind as I drove along the Piedmont streets. P for palatial, plenty, and Protestant. Piedmont has the same kind of gentry that live in Palm Springs, Pasadena, Palos Verdes, and Palm Beach. But I hadn't come to Piedmont for polo and pools, or palaver and pageantry. Putting a pervert in the pokey would have been fun, but I was willing to settle for a few good leads.

The Walters house was on Sea View Avenue, which could just as easily have been called the Street of the Seven Zeroes and then some. Versailles wasn't too far removed from the domains on Sea View. Many of the houses actually did have a view of the Bay, but the greater attraction was the estates themselves. The smallest was large, and the largest was a fiefdom with attendant serfs. Piedmont's plebeians. The cars in the streets didn't belong to the owners, but to the gardeners, and painters, and service people, workers who kept the hedges trimmed, and the gates shiny, and the equipment functioning. You rarely saw an owner from the street, and even then you needed binoculars to make a proper identification.

As Sea View residences went, the Walters house was

nouveau riche, bereft or aged ivy and dusty marble. Their property also lacked the acreage and castlelike edifices of the old guard, but its occupants weren't exactly roughing it. The house was well away from the street, and lined on all sides by a wrought-iron fence. The driveway and the front gate were electrically secured, but I found a phone near the gate that didn't call for change. I lifted the receiver and waited for an answer.

"Yes?"

"I'm Stuart Winter, here to see Mrs. Walters."

The gate buzzed in answer. I hung up the phone and pushed the gate open. I was glad I had worn my comfortable walking shoes. It was a pleasant enough stroll, roses lining the path, and I stopped to smell a few on the long way to the front door. Chimes that went up the scale answered my pressing finger, and the door was opened by a black domestic in uniform.

"Yes?" he asked.

"I'm still Stuart Winter," I said, "and I'm still here to see Mrs. Walters."

I followed a stiff back down a hall and was led to a living room, not *the* living room, but one of several. "Please make yourself comfortable, Mr. Winter," the woman said.

I don't make myself comfortable in the usual ways. I poked around the fancy glossy magazines and coffee table books. I looked at the paintings on the wall and was glad I didn't see any by Vincent. I examined everything in the room, and when I finished I was ready to start on the next room, but the sound of approaching footsteps stayed my snooping.

"Mr. Winter."

"Mrs. Walters."

She held her hand out to me in a horizontal reach. I wasn't sure if I was supposed to shake it or kiss it, so I shook it. I didn't know the etiquette of the situation, which is what happens when a philistine comes to Piedmont. I followed her example and found a seat.

"Would you like some refreshment, Mr. Winter?"

She was the nightingale calling, and I was an answering crow. My velvet voice was years gone, and not even velveteen was left.

"Nothing, thank you."

The servant entered the room, and Mrs. Walters shook her head. Then it was the two of us again. I suppose I should have said how much I admired the room, or the view, or something, but I waited for her. And she didn't know me enough to ask about anything except the thread connecting us, which, after clearing her throat, she did.

"Why don't you tell me how your business is proceeding, Mr. Winter?"

I told her. Went through the picayune details that showed I hadn't left a stone unturned. I had researched jail records, and checked birth records. I had records checked from the coroner's office to marriage records. I had investigated Anita's driving history at the DMV, seeing if in the past six months there had been any vehicle registration, or accident, or driving infraction. I had researched the civil, superior, traffic, and small claims courts, and since Anita was supposed to be politically active, I had even checked with the registrar of voters. All of that had turned up only a pair of worn shoes. My own. I told Mrs. Walters about the witnesses I had interviewed, and finally handed her some typed reports of all my activities and interviews. She barely gave the papers a look.

"Everything you have said and done sounds well and good, Mr. Winter," she said, "but it begs the question. Do you think Anita is still alive?"

I considered hedging, but didn't, and hoped she wouldn't blame the messenger. "There's been no sign of murder, Mrs. Walters. But I think Anita's dead."

She asked me my reasons, and I gave them to her. Our

conversation was calm. Her grief was long past, and my conclusion was just an opinion. An expensive opinion, but she could live with that. I told her I had some leads I was still pursuing, but I needed more of a background on Anita, and she agreed to answer my questions.

"How well do you sign?"

"Fairly well. Anita and I had no problem communicating."

"You took courses?"

"Yes."

"But your husband didn't?"

"He was too busy, he said."

There was the faintest hint of acrimony in her cultured voice.

"Has he always been too busy?"

"Terrence works very hard. I come from a background of wealth, and Terrence doesn't. He always wanted to measure up, and he's worked twice as hard as anyone to do it."

"Has he measured up in your eyes?"

She seemed amused by the question. "He worked very hard at winning me," she said, "twice as hard as anyone else."

"Past tense."

"Poor, poor, pitiful me."

"You only had Anita."

"Yes."

"Does that mean you stopped having relations?"

"Did we ever really start?"

"What do you mean by that?"

"I was avoiding your question. I was trying to be funny. Is your question really necessary?"

"Yes."

"Terrence and I have had separate rooms for some time."

"How long?"

"Fifteen years. Twenty."

"Why your incompatibility? And why'd you stay together?"

"In the beginning it just seemed a matter of our not having enough time together. And then there were—complications."

"Complications?"

She was past the blushing stage, and decided to get blunt. "Terrence found out I was seeing another man."

"When was that?"

"At least fifteen years ago."

"And what happened?"

"He made all sorts of accusations. Claimed he hadn't fathered Anita. But that was ridiculous. And claimed the physical shortcomings of our marriage were my fault. And that was even more ridiculous."

I believed her, didn't even have to stretch my imagination. I wondered how many other men she had entertained over the years, but that wasn't an important concern. I scratched a few words down on paper, and took a moment to look at her eyes. They were dry. "You still haven't told me why you stayed together."

"Maybe we don't know ourselves."

"What kind of a father was he to Anita?"

"Terrence didn't seem very interested in being a father. Sometimes he'd yell at her, think that volume could overcome Anita's deafness."

"And what kind of mother were you?"

"I probably should have spent more time with Anita, but she always had tutors, and a housekeeper who looked after her, and after age twelve she was away at school."

"How did that come about? Her going away to school?"

"It was at Anita's urging, actually. She was rather adamant about leaving."

"And you didn't think that was—suspicious?"

"Suspicious? I don't understand."

I shrugged, and let it pass for a moment. "I understand you're very active socially."

"Yes."

"So you trusted Anita's upbringing to others."

"Yes."

"What would you say if I told you I suspect your husband molested Anita?"

I watched the emotions surface to her face. Her mouth was open, and little sounds of retort kept coming out. It took her several seconds to make a sentence.

"That's ridiculous."

I explained my reasons, told and showed her a few things I had withheld before. I took pieces of her world out, bit by bit, and turned them around, molding them into portraits that weren't very pretty. When I finished, her denials were no longer loud or emphatic. They were more like whimpers.

"I've told you these things," I said, "so that I could ask you one question: could your husband have murdered Anita? Or could he have hired someone to murder her?"

She denied that possibility, and I think she believed what she said, but there were doubts. She was beginning to wonder if she knew her husband at all.

"I want you to look through his belongings," I said, "while I search her room. Look for anything out of the ordinary. See if he wrote her personal checks. See if he might have left notes, anything."

She nodded, but I couldn't be sure she was listening. Then she spoke, but it was more to herself than me. "They say the wife is always the last to know," she said, "but not the mother. The mother should know."

"Mrs. Walters," I said, "please take me to Anita's room."

She led me there, then went away on her own search. I had given her a task, not really expecting she'd find anything, but as something for her fingers to do while her

mind sorted out the shock. I wondered what I'd be thinking if someone showed me naked pictures of a grown
daughter, and then said she was dead; exposed a spouse as
a possible child molester, and then asked me if he was a
murderer. There was a reason for my not being invited to
Piedmont very often.

Anita's room awaited her return. Raggedy Ann and
Andy smiled from atop pink pillows. She didn't keep any
diary, but there was some haiku, and papers, and pictures.
I leafed through a life. It was uneven reading, but that was
Anita. The deaf don't usually write very well. Their vocabulary in most cases is limited, and their sense of syntax
stilted. Anita was not an exception. But I wondered what
jumbled her written thoughts more—her life or her disability.

If I had gone by the book, I would have looked through
Anita's belongings in the beginning of my investigation,
but other leads had detoured me from the obvious. I had
learned a lot of interesting and maybe useless things on
my roundabout way, and now wondered where the hell I
was going.

Tammy Walters finished her search the same time I did.
She hadn't found anything either, even if her face did have
a not very pleasant look of discovery. I had warned her
when we first met about the dangers of cleaning. Sometimes you polish too much and you rub away the veneer.
Maybe it would have been better if I hadn't said anything,
had let her continue in her loveless but decorated marriage. Tammy had hired me to find her daughter, and I was
telling her that the Anita she thought she knew had been
missing from her for quite some time, maybe even a lifetime.

"When does your husband usually get home?" I asked.

"He should arrive any minute," she said.

"I'd like to talk to him in private."

"I'll take you to his den."

I didn't need to leave a breadcrumb trail, but a house with ten rooms and three floors is annoyingly large. It would have been hard not to have privacy in that house. The thought, under the circumstances, was disquieting. I remembered the kind of fact that game shows don't announce: over ninety-five percent of all child molestations occur in the home. For some reason I remember facts like that. I don't have the blessing of selective amnesia.

Terrence Walters's den was much like his office—it was neat and impersonal. The library consisted mostly of legal texts and tomes. I scanned the titles. No *Lolita*. Not even Harold Robbins. And the only subject that hinted of ostentation was an ornately done ship in a bottle. The ship took up one bookshelf. Hanging on the walls were a few framed diplomas, and good citizenship kind of proclamations. Walters's desk was organized, correspondence arranged in several boxes. The drawers were locked, but I picked the locks easily. I rifled his files and found only legal papers, and uninteresting ones at that.

A drafting table stood in the other corner of the den. Terrence Walters was in the process of designing a new garden deck. His lines were very precise, and his writing mechanically straight and spotlessly neat. The planned deck was small and cautious. It would probably go unnoticed, which was undoubtedly how he wanted it.

I wondered at his caution. Was Terrence Walters's den a reflection of his self? I walked to the entry of the room and started my appraisal over again. I checked the lock. It wasn't standard, but had a dead bolt. The door was also a special order, not the pressed or thin wood of most doors, but thick. Voices would be muffled, and ears that tried to pry stymied. I examined his desk. Its less-than-secure locks bothered me. The locks shouldn't have satisfied Walters's cautious nature unless he didn't care about the papers—or unless he had another safe place. I searched for his hidden assurance, and in two minutes I found it, a floor safe. It was fireproof, probably dynamite-proof, and certainly private investigator-proof.

I made another guess, one based on experience. We are an impatient race, especially when it comes to satisfying our vices. The bulk of all valuables, be it drugs or jewelry, are usually secured, but not everything. There is not that much difference between a hoarder and an addict. Be it miser or user, they both have a physical and psychological need for immediate access to their desire. They'll protect the bulk of their investment, but not all. They don't want to wait for tumblers to be clicked, or keys inserted. And Terrence Walters, I thought, was probably a quiet addict. I guessed his vice—or at least one of his vices—was kiddy porn. And while most of the time he would be able to wait to get into his safe, could hold off looking at his hidden booty, there would be moments when he'd have to satisfy his need quickly. I took another look around the room to see what didn't fit.

The room could have passed the marine white-glove test. A maid obviously cleaned and dusted frequently. For a moment I thought about finding the maid and asking if there were any special cleaning requests attached to the room, but I didn't want to run into Terrence Walters on the way. Time was short. I looked for an obvious answer.

And then it came to me. The ship in the bottle. There wasn't any other nautical memorabilia in the room. Putting the fear of God in a maid about harming the ship would have made the shelf it rested on a forbidden area. I removed the bottle and felt around the bookshelf. It seemed solid enough, but my fingers touched on two catches. I loosened the catches, and then removed the shelf backing. A cache had been dug into the wall.

There were three magazines, and a collection of photographs and drawings. One glance was enough. I gathered his collection, and found a manila envelope to house it. I could see him unwinding at the end of the day, a glass of port in one hand, and his kiddy porn in the other. And maybe his memories, his memories of Anita.

I had time enough for some deep breaths, and mentally recited a mantra of "control." Calculated poise is a lawyer's best friend, and I didn't want Terrence Walters to beat me by being more composed. Miss Tuntland always warned me on the phone about my rambunctiousness. "Take a poise pill," she often said. When Terrence Walters walked in the den I was just another shark in a Brooks Brothers suit. But there was some blood in the water.

He tried to look unflappable, but appeared annoyed I was in his domain. "I understand you wanted to see me, Mr. Winter."

He took a seat at his desk, and was able to look down at my position on his couch. All he needed was the black robes.

"Yes," I said. "I called your office yesterday."

"I received your—message. Work demands precluded my calling back."

He was almighty sure of himself. I guessed his wife had said nothing to him yet, or maybe he didn't think I could touch him. I built my case slowly, told him about Anita's quirks. I mentioned her unusual behavior with Darren Fielder, and Will Harrady, and Kevin Bateson. These were indicative, I said, of behavior that resulted from child abuse.

"That's an interesting theory, Mr. Winter," he said, "but one I'm afraid can't be substantiated. And how would we find a culprit? Your list of suspects would be endless— workers in the house, friends, strangers, teachers . . ."

"Even fathers?" I asked.

He stared at me, but showed no emotion. "In an unabridged list," he said, "even that, I suppose, would be possible."

"Will Harrady said Anita hated you."

"That's a rather extreme case of the pot calling the kettle black. Isn't he the teacher who was involved with Anita?"

I was surprised he had heard about that. In court he might have won his case on that question. He would have discredited the witness and the lawyer. He couldn't keep the smugness from his face. I tried to keep my voice level.

"I've kept asking myself why Anita acted like she did," I said, "and the only thing I can come up with is that you sexually abused her."

"That is a very serious accusation," he said, "one you will likely be held accountable for."

"On December thirty-first," I said, "Anita suffered a traumatic experience. She incurred a wound that required many stitches. She was in a state of shock. When she was approached by a man, she thought he was you. And she kept signing, 'Stop it.' And, 'Go away.' And, 'No more.' "

"So what? You said she was in a state of shock. Obviously she didn't know what she was doing."

"Last December Kevin Bateson traumatized your daughter. He slapped her around and then took some photos. Would you like to see them?"

I threw the pictures on his desk, and he looked at them, one by one. His daughter had grown up. She had full breasts, and a pubic patch that told her years. He didn't flinch at the photos, merely looked at them, and then at me.

"I've put those photos in the order in which they taken," I said, "and the interesting thing is that they tell a story. You'll notice her hands in the beginning. I don't think she knew what she was doing, not consciously, but do you know what she's saying?"

He shook his head.

"No, you wouldn't," I said. "You never bothered to learn sign language. What she told the camera is, 'No, Father, no. No more.' I'm willing to bet you've seen those signs before. And probably didn't acknowledge them then either."

"That's ridiculous," he said, but his shirt, stain free after a long day at work, was marked now under his armpits.

I sat and regarded him calmly. And then I threw the manila envelope. It hit his shoulder and face, and one of his magazines spilled out on the desk.

"I found that pile of shit behind your bookshelf," I said. Then I paused, took a moment to get the anger out of my face, and replaced it with my best wolf smile. I patted the bag next to me. "And these I took out of your floor safe."

His face blanched. He shot a look over to the floor, then looked back at me.

"Check it," I said, "check your bookcase too. You won't find anything."

He started to rise, then fell back in his chair.

It was difficult to hear his whisper. "What do you want?"

"I'd like you to stop lying, and tell me the truth."

His breath was drawn, but had started to think again. "Give me what's in your sack."

"Only after I hear what you have to say."

"Then tell me what's in it."

"Why should I?"

The color started coming back to his face, and his breath became more regular. He had paid a lot of money for his safe. He was ready to call my bluff. I had thought it might come to this, had thought about what I would say if it did.

"Why should I give it to you," I said, "when I could hand it over to the DA? Wouldn't he be the one interested in your photographs? And what about your skill with the camera? Everyone thought Kevin Bateson was the first to photograph your daughter. Everyone was wrong, weren't they?"

My guesses worked. His pallor returned with my words. "What do you want to know?"

"How about an easy one for openers: Did you kill Anita?"

"No."

"No? You took advantage of her, abused her, but stopped short of murder. That's right?"

"That's right."

"And you don't know anything about her disappearance?"

"No."

"She was angry. Did she ever threaten to expose you?"

"We've avoided each other for years."

"You didn't answer the question."

"She hated me with her eyes. I was afraid of her, but she never threatened me openly."

"Have you abused any other children?"

"No."

I stared at him, and he must not have liked my look. "I wasn't Anita's father," he said, "Tammy—she had another lover."

"I wondered what you kept telling yourself every time you forced yourself on her," I said. "So that was your line. She's not really my flesh and blood. When did you start abusing her?"

"When she was eight."

"She looked younger in your photos. She looked like she couldn't have been more than four or five."

"She looked young for her age. I swear she was six."

"And this continued?"

"Until she was twelve."

"And I suppose she enticed you? Really wanted to do it? At least you never heard her say she didn't want to, right?"

He started crying, but his tears enraged me. Crocodile or real, I didn't care. And what I hated most was that he hadn't murdered her. Inside I knew that. And if I couldn't make him pay for that crime, and she was dead, there wasn't a hell of a lot more I could do.

I got up, and I didn't realize it, but the sack was in my hand. He didn't miss a beat in his crying, but between sniffles he did point to the bag. He thought his life was walking out of the room, and his repentance went at least that far. "You said you'd give that to me."

He didn't have to ask a second time. When I left the room he was groaning on the ground. That's what happens when you really throw the book at someone. I had put one of his law books in the bag, and I doubt it ever served a better purpose. The tome caught him in his rib cage, threw him from his sat, and when I left he didn't even have the breath to threaten legal action against me.

I stopped to see Tammy Walters before I left. She was sitting in a chair, and staring into space.

"You'll find him in his den," I said. "He's hurting, especially on his left side. He's probably going to need your help to get up. I wouldn't let him up until he tells you something. He has a floor safe. It's in the northwest corner of the room. If you fiddle a bit with the carpet you can see it. Get the combination from him. I suggest a thick instrument in the ribs, one or two of which I think you'll find are broken. I don't think he'll need much persuasion to talk. What you'll find in his safe will sicken you, but it will also get you an uncontested divorce, and a settlement better than the best divorce attorney could ever litigate."

She looked at me, and she understood. She might have understood a little too well. "Don't kill him," I said. "He's not worth it. I want your promise you won't."

She looked at me for a long time, fought with the guilt of her lapsed motherhood, and finally said, "I won't kill him."

Her voice, her pretty voice, was suddenly ugly. I wondered if the change was permanent. I walked to the door, then stopped and turned to Tammy. She was rummaging in the hall closet. I watched her test several umbrellas, but they weren't to her liking. She reached further into the closet and pulled out a cane. From a distance it looked thick, and of substantial wood. Probably oak. Good for walking on treacherous terrain. She took it with her and climbed up the stairs, ready to claim another rib.

I left, not because I didn't want to see him tortured, but because I would have enjoyed it.

17

"Norman," I said, "let's go for a walk."

Norman looked up from his dictating. He was surprised by both my appearance at his office, and my suggestion. His receptionist had waved me by, sure no doubt that he expected me, but he hadn't. He turned off his dictaphone.

A flip remark would have been in order, but Norman refrained. My poker face evidently needed some practice.

"I don't know about a walk, Stuart," he said. "I have some patients later this afternoon."

"We'll be back by then."

"And I have an awful lot of work."

"It's a perfect day for walking."

Norman took a short but pointed glance out a window. The day was grey. It was windy.

"And you're always saying you don't get enough exercise."

"And you've never heard of such a thing as advance notice?"

"That's an excuse."

"I'm not even wearing walking shoes."

"That's another excuse."

"Is there a chance we can do our walking in here?"

Norman is a sneaky fighter. He throws rabbit punches when you least expect them. I answered his question.

"Anita was molested by her father," I said, "from age six to twelve. I confirmed that yesterday."

194

"Let's walk," said Norman.

We didn't say anything for a while, just walked. We left his office on Van Ness and turned on Jackson, hitting the cable car line on Hyde.

"Let's follow the only moving National Historical Landmark in America," I said.

"How about let's ride it," said Norman.

"San Franciscans don't ride the cable cars," I said. "You know that, Norman."

"How far are we walking?"

"That, Norman, I don't know."

He pulled his trench coat a little tighter, and looked a little wistfully at the cable car as it pulled away.

"Do you know what Bernard De Voto said about our city, Norman?"

"I don't even know who Bernard De Voto is."

"He said, 'Make no mistake, stranger, San Francisco is west as all hell.' "

"And what am I supposed to say to that?"

"Maybe you should give O. Henry's line. He said, 'East is east, and west is San Francisco.' "

"It's cold. Are we going to stop for a drink somewhere?"

"Kipling wrote about drinking in San Francisco. He said, 'Drinking is more than an institution. It's a religion.' "

"I'm hearing from everybody but Stuart Winter."

"He's not that quotable."

"Then how about our drinks?"

"They say that most of the landfill for the Embarcadero came from emptied bottles. It's a fact that prohibition merely whetted the City's tongue. Hard liquor became medicinal or religious. Cold medicine was a hundred proof, and Saint's days occurred three or four times a week until the Volstead Act was repealed. And then the saints were forgotten but saints keep well."

"Stuart, do you want to talk about Anita?"

"Not yet, Norman. Not yet."

"When do you think you'll want to?"

"Maybe by the time we reach Telegraph Hill."

Norman groaned. Loudly.

"Fear not, Norman. Your historical guide is here."

"How about I flag us a cab. We must be talking close to twenty blocks."

"We both need it, Norman. Your stomach, my mind."

"Your point's well taken."

"Are we having fun yet?"

"No."

"We're supposed to be. This is the Queen City of the Pacific, double entendre not intended. In days of old they said San Francisco's front gates were pearly, and its streets were gold. But for fun you went to the back alleys, the byways where the smoke drifted from opium dens, and waiting where that smoke drifted were the whores who hawked and practiced their trade in cribs that were the scourge of the world."

"That doesn't sound so marvelous."

"Do I hear echoes of a bluenose credo? Bluenoses never liked the fact that San Franciscans didn't sin in darkness, and they still don't. The self-proclaimed righteous have always said God was going to judge against this city. When the 1906 earthquake struck, those who thought they stood next to God said He had come calling on San Francisco. But do you know what Charles Field said?"

"I don't know who the hell Charles Field was."

"Field wrote:

> *'If as they say, God spanked the town,*
> *For being over frisky,*
> *Why did he burn his churches down,*
> *And spare Hotaling's whiskey?'*

Answer Field's question, Norman."

"Maybe the devil has a thirst."

"And maybe God has a special place in his heart for drunks, fools, and Americans. That's a trinity I know better than most, Norman."

We didn't say much else on the way to Telegraph Hill. We walked quickly and determinedly to a location where feet serve better than unwanted cars. They don't allow commuter parking on the hill. Those that made it to the top of the hill decided they didn't want to be inconvenienced by the cars of those who hadn't made it. Norman was huffing and puffing by the time we reached the crest.

We looked around. Once Telegraph Hill was a signaling ground, a place where semaphore flags announced to the merchants and the interested citizenry the arrival of ships in the Golden Gate. Today the view is still unequaled, even if the only waving these days is for cabs or cameras. We looked around, took in the view, and Norman finally caught his breath.

"Talk, goddamn you," he said.

"While we walk," I said.

He had to catch up to me, and when he did I didn't give him time to complain. "Anita was used and abused by just about everyone," I said. "It got me down. I told myself I'd take today off and that I wouldn't think about it. But that made me think about it more. You're always saying I never open up. You're always saying I internalize. So I decided to stop by."

"And quite literally to share the pain."

"Sometimes the mouth bone's connected to the feet bones."

"And sometimes, Stuart, it's connected to the butt bone."

We talked about the case. It interested Norman enough to silence his complaints all the while we walked on Montgomery Street. He didn't remember his aching feet until we hit California. I suppose I felt better for talking. Mostly, I just recited facts, but their mention made me breathe a little easier, even if I didn't know why. Norman's feet slowed until he said he couldn't walk another step. We stopped at Old St. Mary's Church on California and Grant. Since 1854 San Franciscans have been admonished by the lettering on the church: SON OBSERVE THE TIME AND FLY FROM EVIL. Norman noticed the inscription.

"Good advice for you," he said. "Time you left your trade. It's not healthy."

"Someday," I said.

"Flag us a cab, will you? Or carry me to the cable car stop."

"I'll watch for a cab. But you picked a good resting spot."

"How's that?"

"Joshua Abraham Norton died on the spot near where you're sitting in January 1880."

"Somehow that's not comforting. But I suppose you're going to tell me who Joshua Abraham Norton was."

I nodded, but didn't start the telling right away. You wonder at stories, whether they can be as marvelous as they seem. The patina of time often leaves a gentler surface, one that you aren't anxious to scrape away, but Joshua Abraham Norton passed any scrubbing test. He was the real article, one of those San Francisco legends that you don't want to fade away, the kind worth a telling and retelling. Norton's was a riches to rags to rich rags story.

"Norton arrived in San Francisco in 1849," I said. "He wasn't just another sourdougher. He had money, and his fortune increased, but he got greedy. In 1854 he attempted to corner the rice market. The move backfired and left him a pauper. He next surfaced in 1859 when he walked into the *San Francisco Bulletin* and left his calling card, a written announcement that proclaimed himself as Norton I,

Emperor of the United States. The *Bulletin* decided it was a good joke. They printed his proclamation, the first of many. And that was the start of Norton I's twenty-one-year reign."

"So he was the town joke?" said Norman.

"He started that way," I said, "as the kind of joke that usually draws derisive laughter, but somehow the joke evolved and turned into an example of good humor, and there is a difference, if few precedents."

"You almost sound sentimental, Stuart."

"I am. And so were the people of San Francisco. They took Norton to their hearts. They courted his patronage, and even listened to his ideas. He demanded a huge Christmas tree be brought to Union Square as a holiday offering to the children of San Francisco, and it was, and is, to this very day."

Norman still looked skeptical. "Don't tell me the people didn't laugh at him during his reign," he said. "I know human nature better than that."

"They did," I said. "Some of his proclamations were ridiculous. He proposed funds for a bridge connecting San Francisco with Oakland, and later, just when the laughs were dying, he said that the Golden Gate should also be spanned by a bridge. He cabled the leaders of the world and proposed peace, and that was always good for a laugh, too."

"You make him sound like he wasn't a comic figure."

"I don't mean to. He was funny, a ridiculous little figure in epaulets, but he had such spirit. Norton was invited to major and minor ceremonies throughout the City. He often journeyed to Sacramento to make his will known to the state legislature, as if politicians weren't comic enough by themselves. But wherever Norton went, he had a special way of making his own points and statements. At one gathering he was sitting on the speaker's platform when anti-Chinese riots broke out. With violence all around,

Norton stood up and recited the Lord's Prayer. They say the riots stopped as quickly as they had begun."

Norman listened a little more attentively. "Did our Emperor have a court?" he asked.

"Two companions named Bummer and Lazarus, and the blood royal certainly didn't flow through their vein. They were mutts, unmistakably ugly mutts, that Norton rescued from death. They followed him everywhere, and became celebrated royalty in their own way. They sat next to Norton at opening night theatre performances."

"In a royal box, I suppose?"

"Or reserved seats. And the audience always made a point of rising to their feet when the Emperor and his two companions entered to their seats."

"At this point I'll rise for a cab and nothing else," said Norman. "Flag one, Stuart."

I raised my hand to two passing cabs. They chose to ignore it. I kept watch for more.

"You can look and talk at the same time, can't you? Tell me more about the Emperor."

"There are lots of stories, Norman. But I just got you your cab."

Norman struggled to his feet as a taxi inched along through traffic.

"When Bummer died they say more than 10,000 people marched in his funeral procession His death prompted front-page obituaries, and eulogies from leading writers and citizens. But the dog turned out to be merely a reflection of his owner. Norman's death in 1880 brought 30,000 people out to mourn, the largest funeral the City had ever seen. The flags of California flew at half mast, and I think a little of San Francisco's heart was buried with our Emperor."

"Get in, Stuart."

"I think I have a little more walking to do."

"Then call me later."

"I will. Thank you, Norman."

I wondered why there was no statue to Norton, no plaque. Maybe he was too hard to explain.

There was still some life left in my legs. Later I knew I'd pay the price. I continued up California and stopped at the Masonic Arts Temple. The placards announced that *Secret Societies* would open in two weeks. I decided I wanted a sneak preview.

A woman, probably a frustrated understudy, barred my entrance. She snapped her gum at me and said, "The rehearsals are closed."

"Then could you take a note to Goldilocks for me?" I asked. "She told me to stop by, and I'd hate to miss her. If you like, I'd be glad to watch the door for you."

I said everything very quickly, and very sincerely. I had a smile on my face, and a puppy-dog manner. The guard's gum snapping became a little less pronounced.

"Okay," she finally said, "but make sure you stay out of sight while I deliver the note. It could be my job."

"Thank you," I said, already writing. My note was short, and I didn't bother to fold it. It merely told Goldilocks that her favorite private dick was waiting outside to take her for drinks.

I handed my note over, offered a little more gratitude, then stepped inside and waited for my messenger to walk out of sight. I moved quietly to the back of the theater, but my steps weren't as stealthy as the two cat characters on stage. I couldn't follow what was going on, except that at first they fought, then they made love, and then the two actions couldn't be separated. But their entwinement became *cattus interruptus* when a fire leapt out of a garbage can; it spewed flame and ashes at the cats and outhissed them until they backed off with electric cries and electric eyes, their backs and tails charged and inflated.

The fire died, but the garbage can didn't settle. It bounced and tilted, shook and shimmied, spewing beer cans and rotten eggs and offal all over the stage in what I suppose advertised the birth pains of a city, but what does a city birth? I watched a figure emerge, a figure that was a living fire in a sequined flame costume. Snakelike, Goldilocks undulated from the garbage can, a self-birth that lifted her out of the fire. She was the pristine vision amid the filth. But somehow it was clear her character wouldn't remain untainted for long.

A bass voice called for lights, and Vincent came on stage. He started talking, not loud enough for me to hear him, but close enough for me to decide I should leave. I didn't know whether Goldilocks could get away to see me, or even wanted to, but I decided to wait no more than a half-hour. The doorwoman relieved me at my post, so I went outside and sat on the curb. My patience surprised me by running to the better part of an hour, and it was finally rewarded, in a manner of speaking, by Goldilocks.

She was in some kind of costume, but not by much. She wore leather spiked gloves, a black halter top, and a black skirt. She wasn't wearing a bra, and buxom as she was, there didn't appear to be any need, save propriety, and that wasn't in her wardrobe. Stiletto heels were obligatory for her outfit, and they were accented by snakeskin hosiery. I stared at her legs for several seconds. She obliged my look with a model's turn.

"Poisonous or nonpoisonous?" I asked.

"Depends on the snake," she said.

She moved her hand up and down the fabric. "I like to slither in and out of them," she said.

I don't know why I started the conversation, but habit made me try for the last word. "Let's go get our venom," I said.

She hissed, but I still walked with her.

"I figured I'd hear from you," she said while we walked.

"Why?" I said. "Just one look, that's all it took?"

"Do you want another?"

"Curiosity killed the cat. Even those cats tangoing on stage knew to run from you."

"You saw?"

She sounded pleased. I nodded, but didn't comment, just opened the door for her, let her lead and draw all the attention. There were plenty of empty booths, but she chose a table in the middle of the place. I gave our orders to the bartender, who had more eyes for Goldilocks than his pour. At about a seven count he eased up. I asked for a couple of large water backs, carried the drinks to the table, and commented on the pour.

"When I have a thirst I ought to bring you along," I said.

"What do you do when you don't have a thirst?"

I thought of a few answers, all of them obscene, then decided to get serious. "Are you always acting?"

"Isn't everybody?"

"I don't know," I said, "but when I talk with you I feel you're performing. So I have to wonder, is this is you, or is it that actress called Goldilocks talking?"

"I'm a Gemini. But the two selves have fused. I'm me. I used to worry about being able to turn it off, but now I don't. I'm turned on all the time."

"There you go again."

She laughed at me, making me feel like a bit of a stick in the mud, and I could see her point, so I smiled back. Then she stopped laughing, and appraised me.

"So," she said, "did you come to court me, or do you still want to know about that deaf girl?"

"Today's a business call," I said.

She gave a loud mock-sigh. "Interrogate me," she said. "Beat me, even. But do it in about ten minutes."

"Are you the jealous type, Goldilocks?"

"No. I'm confident. If I don't hold a man's attention, then he's blind."

"Or maybe deaf?"

"Or maybe I'm holding something else."

She gave me her teasing smile, but I didn't soften my glance, so she pouted.

"If you're trying to ask whether I was threatened by that deaf girl," she said, "I wasn't. Vincent and I weren't really together any more when she came along. Not that we didn't see each other now and again. We did and we do. But I've never been ready to parade in white with him, and never will."

"You're still intimate, then?"

"Infrequently."

"Why?"

"Why infrequently? Or why not more frequently?"

"Either."

"We're good for each other in bed, but not out of it. We play off our fantasies."

"Tell me about them."

"Are you a voyeur?" she asked.

"I'm curious," I said.

She gave me a look that was supposed to make me go weak at the knees, then accented it with licking lips. "When we fuck we're not afraid to assume different roles. We play scenes."

"So you're an actress in bed, too?"

"And an acrobatress on a mattress."

"Let's get back to you and Vincent."

"We're kinky together."

"So you've said. Does your loveplay ever get violent?"

"I suppose."

"You suppose?"

"Vincent can get very intense. But I know how to channel his stream."

"What if someone didn't know how to channel his stream?"

Goldilocks shrugged.

"When Vincent's intense, what kind of demands does he make?"

"It depends on who he is at the moment."

"I've heard that Vincent's frightened some of his models. I've also heard he's scared away some bed partners."

"So what?"

"Has Vincent ever lost himself with you? Become so involved, so intense, you couldn't reach him?"

Goldilocks wasn't used to being unsettled. Her hand was unsteady when she pulled out a cigarette, or maybe she made it shake. Maybe she was that good an actress.

"What are you driving at?"

"Answer the question."

She lit the cigarette, and inhaled. She blew the smoke at me. "He's lost it a few times. But that just made it more exciting."

"Tell me about those times."

"Why should I?"

"To humor me."

She inhaled her cigarette again, fully inflated her lungs, which drew every glance in the bar, then exhaled.

"A few times he got into a character he couldn't release from too quickly."

"Which translates into what?"

"Good times."

"And?"

"Maybe I got thrown around a little."

"Hit?"

"Some."

"Injured?"

"I never needed to go to the hospital or anything . . ."

"Hurt?"

"Maybe a little . . ."

"So he is dangerous. Probably unbalanced. Did he ever threaten to kill you?"

"It was all acting!"

Her shout turned every head. Goldilocks didn't care.

"That's all it was—acting."

"But he did threaten you sometimes?"

"And I threatened him. It was spice. And cleaner than the mind games you're playing now."

Goldilocks finished her drink, and stamped out her cigarette. "I have to get back," she said.

"I'll walk you."

"Don't bother. And don't call on me again about this case. It bores me. Not everybody's a murderer, you know. Your little chippy is probably off somewhere having a good time."

"I hope so," I said, and I was sincere, but Goldilocks didn't much give a damn about that. The scene called for her to walk off without a good-bye, and she played it to the hilt.

I didn't really know what my cue was, so I paid attention to my drink, and started to make my notes. I ignored the low murmurs. I wrote down our dialogue as best I remembered, and thought back to what she had said about Vincent's threats.

Spice, she had called them.

Sugar and spice, and everything nice. That's what little girls are made of.

18

"IT'S GOOD TO HEAR your voice, Miss Tuntland."

"And it's rare to hear yours, Mr. Winter."

Miss Tuntland's rebuff wasn't much of one. I knew I'd been short with her lately, not keeping her up to date with the case. She never liked to be left out.

"You wouldn't believe the last few days."

"Maybe I would if you told me about them."

"How many ways are there to say 'dead end'? I don't happen to have my thesaurus handy."

"Oh. And is Ellen Reardon a 'dead end'?"

When you don't have a ready retort, you go on the defensive. "How can a voice as sweet as yours have so many cynical edges?"

"It's from the snake oil someone keeps trying to shove down my throat."

"It beats hosiery."

"Which means what?"

"I just met with Goldilocks. She was dressed like a spitting cobra and lived up to her outfit. I learned Vincent is a possibly dangerous kink. Part of the general trend."

"Which is?"

"Which is not a pretty trend. Vincent doesn't even head the list of kinks. Anita was sexually abused for years by her father, the esquire Terrence Walters."

I listened to her sigh. It was real. Maybe I called her to

hear those sighs. Maybe I needed to know there was one person in the world who really cared.

"And remember Kevin Bateson?"

"The photographer?"

"That and other things. One day he took the time to beat Anita, and her dignity wasn't the only thing he stripped. She's on parade in one of this month's girlie papers. And he was a friend. Should I tell you about another friend?"

"Yes."

"Dr. William Henry Harrison. The reverend, the venerable, Dr. Harrison. He lied about an injury Anita received at the Gorilla Project. He covered up her injury to protect his hairy babes. And I guess I shouldn't forget mentioning another one of her friends—Joseph, poor Joseph. He grabbed her ear, hurt her, but at least he felt bad about it. I'm sure it was accidental, but I think Anita just saw it as one last betrayal. Couldn't even count on Joseph her friend, Joseph the gorilla. She had learned not to trust humans, and that included herself. I don't think she liked that, but she didn't have a hell of a lot of good examples to learn from."

"You don't paint a very pretty picture."

"Maybe it's one I should suggest to Vincent. Maybe he could make a grand mural and call it the 'Revelations of Winter.' He could show me in action over the past few days, sharing drinks with bag people and talking to confused models. Or maybe it should be a 'connect the dots' kind of project. Follow the trail of Winter's walks and talks and maybe you can piece together Anita's body. But I'm rambling, aren't I, Miss Tuntland? We're not talking about a painting, we're talking about a lot of dark corners. But there—that's another idea. How about a display of a lot of dark corners, and Anita's hands captioning what's going on in sign language? Her hands are great explainers. You should have seen them explaining away in her nude photos. 'Stop it,' she kept signing. To her father, to

Bateson, to Joseph even. Maybe that's what she'd be signing to me now."

"Stop it," said Miss Tuntland.

I didn't know whether she was repeating my words, or telling me to quit, but I decided hers was the voice of Anita, and so I did stop it. I was tired of the whole dirty thing, anyway.

"What are you going to do now?"

Miss Tuntland used her concerned voice, and it disarmed even my self-pity.

"I don't know," I said. "I've been presuming her death for the past few days. Maybe I'm wrong about that. Maybe she did just up and leave."

"And if she didn't?"

"Not a hell of a lot of people seem to care either way."

"Does that mean you're giving up?"

"You know better than that."

"Yes, I do."

"I'm sweating out inspiration now. I thought I'd pant a little for you. Didn't someone say investigation was ninety-nine percent perspiration and one percent inspiration?"

"Thomas Alva Edison. And he said it about genius, not investigating. If I'm to believe the gospel according to Winter, investigating is ninety-nine percent desperation."

"Which leaves me with a whole one percent to work on."

"What are you and your percent going to do now?"

"This is the part in the conversation where I should break down, Miss Tuntland. Where I should tell you the bloodhound has run out of scent. Where you're supposed to pat me on the head and say, 'Good doggie' anyway. Tomorrow's the first day I don't have anyplace to go, no clues to follow up."

"Good doggie," she said. "Now shoo."

"What?"

"It's not the end of the world. Maybe you need to work on something else. Maybe you need a break."

"That sounds familiar. I keep telling myself the same thing. I woke up this morning and said I wasn't going to work on the case. Said I was just going to walk and breathe, but it didn't work. I'm not ready to let go, not yet."

"Even if you're holding a tiger's tail?"

"Especially then."

"You were probably a stubborn little boy."

"No, I was smarter then. Better natured."

"So what happened?"

"I discovered there was no Tooth Fairy. No Santa Claus. And learned that love doesn't conquer all, and hate doesn't sustain you."

"Is that a violin I hear playing over the line?"

"No. Muzak."

"Thought so."

"But I'm glad you heard the elevator ride out."

"It wasn't a very long ride. And I still think we're going up."

There was a little pause. Between the cuteness there had been real human openings. That's always scary. I retreated from that border. "Thanks," I said.

"I'm glad you called," she said.

"So am I. But I never even asked you if there were any messages."

"Just one. From a secret admirer. She said to take care."

"If she calls back, tell her I will. And tell her the same."

"Good-bye."

"Bye."

When you get a little warmth in your stomach, sometimes you get greedy, and want a little more. So I reached once again for the phone, and in a few short minutes got myself invited over to Ellen's.

I stopped for a good bottle of wine, and didn't spare either the expense or the gas. I was out of the City quickly, and onto the Bay Bridge. I careened around Lake Merritt, didn't even stop to rubberneck the interesting birds that are usually there, and found a parking space near Ellen's place. When I pushed her doorbell I saw flashing lights strobe inside, but the show didn't last long. She was at the door, and then in my arms. We didn't waste words. There was a hunger in us that preceded decorum by about three million years.

Our lovemaking started quickly, but it wasn't a dash we wanted, but a moment to never end. I entered her, and she entered me. At first I tried to conduct our love. I moved my hands along her taut body, licked the sweat and dampness on her thighs, and kissed her nipples, but she could feel the orchestration in my movements, and she didn't want that. It wasn't a night for rote lovemaking, but for acting on what felt good. We followed impulses and feelings. We moved, and bucked, and cried, and neither of us could be sure who was pushing, and grabbing, and breathing, and moaning.

Unity, so hard to reach, and so brief, leaves suddenly. When the lights and flashes and shakes have finished, when the bed stops shaking and you've fallen to separate pillows, there is that return to self. Ellen's consciousness came back a few seconds after mine. She didn't try to rationalize, or verbalize; she just reached for me. It was better landing arm in arm, hugging and holding while all our tremors and twitches stopped. Our breathing slowed together. My arm was under her back, my hand resting on her warm breast. We pretended we weren't really going to sleep, that we were just resting up for more fun and games, but it would have been anticlimactic to climb and fall from Everest more than once in a night, or maybe even a lifetime.

With her warmth at my side, I expected I'd find Ellen in my dreams, but dreams aren't made that way. I slept deeply for a few hours, the slumber of death that comes after offering life, and on the path of the dead I found Anita. It was almost the same dream as before. Anita tried to tell me who murdered her, kept signing a name, and I yelled at her to speak.

"Goddammit, you dummy! Tell me the name."

And her face, just as angry as her hands, signed back at me, cursing my stupidness probably, certainly.

I awoke back on the long path to nowhere. My hands were trembling, and I was cold.

It was very dark. I couldn't see my hands in front of me, the hands I was trying to mold into the sign of her murderer. I thought about signing, about hand words, and how the deaf sometimes unconsciously signed. And I remembered that even the hearing who didn't know sign language sometimes unconsciously signed. On Martha's Vineyard they had done that.

Which reminded me of something. And then my breath left me. I shook Ellen, started yelling questions at her, then remembered to turn on the light.

She was groggy. Her hearing aids were on the nightstand, and she fumbled with them, finally getting them in. At first she couldn't understand what I was asking. But I kept repeating the same question over and over.

"What is the sign for murderer?"

She showed me. It was a sign I had seen many times. And it told me who had murdered Anita.

19

I DIDN'T REALLY FEEL very smart. The answer had been in front of my eyes for a very long time. A deaf private investigator, any deaf person, would have seen it. Vincent had used everything but fireworks to announce his crime. With his hands he broadcast that he was a murderer, shouted out his admission in sign language.

And no one had heard him.

I had thought it affectation, or a tic, the movement of his index finger on his right hand, the pushing forward and slashing moving under his left palm. He carried his blood letter openly, and it made me wonder about Anita's last moments. She must have known she was dying, and with her last strength signed at him, over and over, murderer—murderer—murderer. It was a curse she left on him, a curse that played on him, and made him unconsciously repeat her hand movements, and tell the world her last word.

But his announcement wasn't the kind of evidence that would hold up in court. I drove to China Basin to find the kind of evidence that would.

"Okay, Anita," I said, "where do I look?" But she didn't answer. It wasn't dreamtime yet. So I listened to the hum of the Olds, and looked out at the darkness, and fiddled with the controls of my mind, changing station after station in search of the right information.

"About ten years ago he changed his name to Vincent.

Everyone guesses the name comes from Vincent Van Gogh, but our Vincent doesn't talk about it."

"He fantasizes out loud, fantasizes about weird things."

"He ejaculated into a cup and mixed his semen with red paint."

"Vincent is a slave to art. It commands me."

"He cut himself, quite deeply, and let his blood mix with the paint."

"Two of your paintings interested me, Mr. Patchen."

The unflappable Vincent had been bothered by those words. Why? He had provided witnesses who corroborated that he had paid Anita for the faucet handle and the cabinet door. But in my mind's crystal test something wasn't chiming right.

"Vincent can get very intense. But I know how to channel his stream."

"Vincent needed her for evaluation purposes, needed someone without ears."

"Sometimes he puts me off balance."

"He's lost it a few times. But that just made it more exciting."

"Vincent doesn't believe in waste. He likes his oddments. That's what he calls them. He doesn't believe in waste. He makes sculptures and decorative pieces from absolute junk, things just lying around. He's got a thing against throwing stuff away. He's sort of obsessed about getting a use out of everything, even discards."

I stopped. Something was trying to make itself heard. I drove along Townsend and again parked in front of Maxilla & Mandible. The night brought a phosphorescent glow to the bones, their whiteness standing out in the gloom. The darkness was more their element, which is not to say it made them look better. The hard edges of death aren't sanitized in shadows like they are under decorator lights. They urged those who still had skin on their bones to keep walking.

Everything was quiet and dark, and my steps sounded overloud while I walked down the alleyway. There wasn't even enough light to read the graffiti.

I circled around the back, walked to the long-deserted train tracks to make sure no one was around, then returned to the alley and Vincent's loft.

The door wasn't unlocked this time, and I didn't have the patience to try and pick the locks. I took my coat off, broke a window, and got inside quickly. It would have been just my luck to have a chance black-and-white come along. Asking for my license to be revoked meant I was playing with my pulse and not my mind. It wasn't smart, but I told myself it was necessary.

My flashlight came out as I climbed the creaky stairs. In the back of my mind I regretted not carrying a gun in my trunk for just such an occasion, but I've never been really comfortable holding hardware. I came to the fire door, and shoved it open. It cried out for oiled tracks. I shone my light inside, took a few tentative steps, and decided more light would serve me better than caution. I found a wall switch.

I kicked around a lot of trash, and nosed about some corners, but I kept angling for the storage shed. On my last visit it had been clean and empty, had even smelled clean, and in the midst of all the refuse any cleanliness made me suspicious. A lock barred entry to the shed, a lock that resisted my efforts. I found some metal rods on the floor, made several misguided attempts with brute strength, then rigged up a fulcrum with the rods. Vincent was right. His oddments did have purpose. Aided by curses, physics, and a couple of hundred pounds, the lock finally gave.

There were twelve paintings in the shed. I brought them out to the light. All had been on display the weekend before. I wondered why these twelve had returned, while looking at them closely.

Maybe there is a sixth sense. Maybe sixth sense is nothing more than your unconscious mind knocking on your conscious with a message. But two of the twelve paintings I kept coming back to. I even remembered their titles from the show: 'I Need Her,' and 'The Plastic Surgeon's Mistress.'

I placed the paintings on top of the shed and looked at them side by side. There didn't seem to be anything that tied them together, save their bizarreness. I turned them around, viewed them from different angles, close up and from a distance.

'I Need Her' kept drawing my attention. Maybe I was attracted to puns. It should have been titled 'I Knead Her.' The hands were kneading the naked woman, the graphically naked woman without the head. I tested the pubic hairs which looked so real, and they felt real. I wondered if they were Vincent's contributions, or whether he had plucked them from a model.

'I Need Her.' I said the name outloud. It didn't taste quite right, I said it again, a little more quickly. I Need Her. INeedHer.

Anita.

The body looked familiar now also. There was a triple meaning to Vincent's title. He probably had needed her. And kneaded her. Anita.

Everyone said Vincent didn't believe in waste. He liked to see his oddments. And Anita was just another oddment. In death he had used her for a last painting. Take, paint, this is her body. I wondered how far his inspiration had extended, whether he had taken an epidermal layer and painted over that, or just snipped some pubic hairs. It was Anita on canvas, maybe too literally. I was sure of that.

I was on a grisly roll, and looked at the second painting and waited for revelations. How had Anita contributed to 'The Plastic Surgeon's Mistress?' Everyone's first glance was at the wife's wound. Vincent would have known that. And what I judged was that the trickling design of blood was too lifelike, too inspired. Under the paint would be found Anita's blood, covered over and covered up, but there for Vincent to know. He probably wouldn't have painted over the blood if it hadn't been necessary, but blood pales and turns to rust when it stops flowing. So Vincent had added some paint. I looked at the pool of blood at the woman's feet. The knife had fallen there also, but it didn't look so much like a throwing knife as a painter's tool, the kind that's used to scrape paint from palettes. And there was a reflection I noticed for the first time from the pool of blood. It wasn't the knifethrower's wife, for she faced her husband. It was Anita.

I had to step away from the paintings, Vincent's testimonials to murder. It's not the kind of thing you can prepare for. It made me a little weak, and a little careless, made me want to not think about everything that had happened. But the dominos kept clicking, or was it bones that were rolling? It was clear the murder had excited him. Her seeping life inspired his art. And while she was dying, while she bled to death, he had probably thrown a canvas or two under her to capture the escaping remains of her life. Maybe he hadn't meant to kill her, but in death he had used her.

"You will not move."

I almost laughed. And it almost was comic. Entrances and lines like that went out with black-and-white movies. But a very black gun was centered on me, and Vincent's very white teeth were smiling.

"I was in the neighborhood," I said, my answer quick, if not sure. "I saw someone had broken in your place. Looks like they wanted to get your paintings. Maybe I scared them off."

"Move back," he said, and then signed murderer. Unconsciously. But I believed him, and moved back.

"I don't know if they got away with any paintings," I said. "There are only twelve left."

Vincent was standing where I had stood. He was alternately looking at me, and at the two paintings. I waited for him to pay more attention to his works, or put down his gun, but he didn't seem interested in doing either.

"Twelve paintings?" he asked. "Then why were you interested in only these two?"

And then he signed again. Murderer.

"They were up there. Like I said, I probably scared the thieves away . . ."

"Those interesting thieves who just happened to put aside these two paintings, these paintings you were so curiously interested in. I thought you didn't like Vincent's paintings."

I put on a silly grin, and started edging toward the door. "That from someone who really doesn't know anything about art . . ."

"Stop moving, Mr. Winter. Vincent knows how to use this gun, and he won't hesitate. You've given Vincent the perfect excuse to kill you, and I haven't yet thought of a reason I shouldn't accept your offer. Vincent came to his loft. There were signs of a break in. Vincent happened to be carrying some protection, for this isn't the safest area, and regretfully used his protection when he was attacked in his studio. Vincent defended himself. Do you want to die now?"

"No."

"Then tell a tale, Scheherazade."

"Is that how you'll paint me? As Scheherazade?"

Murderer, he signed. His right hand, his gun hand, moving.

"That's a clever idea."

"Because I'd hate to just be taken down to the morgue. That is, if you have to shoot me."

"Your discoveries don't give Vincent a choice. I watched you. You saw those paintings for what they are. You know."

His gun was getting too centered. I had to keep him talking. "I imagine Anita was grateful that you immortalized her death. She probably even participated."

"She didn't. She was most churlish."

Murderer, he signed.

"Didn't she understand?"

"No. Vincent explained to her. Told her he needed her ears. You remember Van Gogh, don't you? How he gave up his ear to a woman?"

"Yes."

"Vincent found Anita on New Year's Eve. It was unexpected. But when I saw her damaged ear, I knew what I was called upon to do. I took her to the studio, and then asked for her offering. She didn't use her ears anyway, and I wanted them."

"And what did she say?"

"She didn't understand. She never understood. Whenever Vincent painted her, he talked with her. Vincent told her things, beautiful things, and she never heard. She wanted Vincent to face her, to explain, but Vincent couldn't do that. I knew our time would come."

"You weren't lovers?"

"Our bond was deeper than that. She was meant for Vincent."

Murderer, he signed.

"You took her ear?"

"Vincent took both of them. Vincent surpassed Van Gogh."

"But she fought you?"

"She didn't understand. Vincent tried to explain, but she wouldn't listen. So Vincent held her throat until she didn't move, and then he gathered her ears."

"But she wasn't dead yet, was she?"

"She awakened for a little while—afterwards."

"And you already had the canvases under her?"

"Yes."

"And what did she do?"

Murderer, he signed.

Vincent measured me with his eyes. "Her blood was so vital, so inspiring, Scheherazade."

"How will you use me?" I asked.

"Like the Sultan used his maidens. He killed them."

"All except Scheherazade," I said. "Her stories enchanted him, her stories lived on forever, like I should."

Vincent was skeptical. "You are not the type to willingly give your life to art. You are selfish."

"Selfish enough to want to live forever. With my blood as your oil, I might."

Vincent rubbed his beard with his left hand. "Yes," he said, "you might."

I kept talking. I knew the moment I wanted, but he had to be nearer.

"But if I have to die," I said, "I want an active death. I want my life fluid to spurt out, not to be collected from the floor. I'd rather live, but that's not possible, is it?"

"No, it's not."

"Then set up the canvases near to me. Shoot me so that I may paint my own story."

Vincent was getting excited. "Yes," he said. "Vincent is inspired. Vincent will use you in a painting. Vincent will call it 'Light Bearer,' and you will be Prometheus who brought us fire. And the fire will be blood red, and it will be you."

Murderer, he signed.

Vincent motioned me with his gun hand to a point in the loft away from the windows and the exit, and then he readied himself for my red painting. He decided my last testaments would be on two canvases. I wasn't going to go out six foot down, but on measurements five foot by seven, and four foot by three. I watched my shrouds being stretched and prepared from across the room. He worked with the gun next to his hand, his labors rote, his eyes more on me than his canvases. Vincent finished quickly, set up the canvases next to some pillars, then repositioned me with his gun. I did the .44 shuffle, the waving sights moving me right and left, until finally I was where he wanted me, even if my canvases weren't. He told me not to move, not even to breathe, and I believed in his words, and his gun hand. He was off to my right, working with his left hand, but his attention wasn't divided. He moved the canvases by feel. I knew he'd get no closer.

"Vincent," I asked softly, "what did Anita say to you when she awakened for the first time?"

Murderer, he began to sign, his gun moving forward and twisting under his left palm.

With the sign of his guilt, I ran at him. And just as his hand and gun were tilted, my long leg kicked at his crotch. He tried to hurry the gun along, tried to finish his work and shoot me, but my hand found his face first. As he fell back I hit him once more, a chop on his forearm. He dropped the gun.

It fell between the two of us, but I was the only one standing. I grabbed it from the floor, and then he lunged at my leg. He wrenched my knee, and tried to bring me down. I was given an instant to make a decision, and I did.

I tell myself there was only one decision, that I couldn't have taken the chance of just hitting his head with the gun. I had but an instant to act, even if that instant was enough to think and deliberate about all of the possibilities at hand. I chose the possibility in hand.

I shot him through the back of his neck.

He had several moments more of life, and took them to face me, and stare me in the eye.

And then he signed murderer at me, and died.

20

THE POLICE WANTED STATEMENTS, and more statements. I gave them most of what they wanted, leaving a few closets closed, including one or two of mine. There were some people I didn't want bothered, and a few facts that wouldn't look good for a PI, so I gave the truth according to Winter, which wasn't the whole truth and nothing but the truth, but it was close enough.

The press was stirred up. It was a headline writer's dream, and promised to be good play for days. Vanishing wilderness, acrid rain, and diminished quality of life aren't stories people want to read when compared to murder. And so the media waited around for the bits and pieces that came out, and that's what they got.

The police were still questioning me at the station when they found Anita's ears. They were in Vincent's freezer at his home. Her ears, and lab analysis of the two paintings, legitimized my story.

I told the police about Vincent's penchant for "oddments," and how I suspected they might find parts of the rest of Anita's body in some deep freeze. They said they would pursue my theory, and finally released me, but not without the familiar spiel about my being available for further questioning.

I successfully avoided the press by staying at Norman Cohen's house. He was between wives, and had an extra room. I pretended to be asleep when he arrived home, and slipped out when he finally retired. I wasn't ready for sleep yet.

I kept telling myself I was stupid, that the case was over. But I didn't want to sleep, because I knew Anita would still be in my dreams. And I knew when I asked her who her murderer was, she wouldn't sign Vincent. She—or my subconscious—never had.

Sergeant Don Bryant wasn't too pleased to hear from me at midnight, but he owed me, and made good on his debt. I picked him up and we drove to Vincent's home on Pacific Heights. Our conversation was brief. He knew about the day's events, but didn't ask me about them, didn't even ask why I wanted to go to Vincent's house.

"Why didn't you call me earlier?" he asked.

"Two reasons," I said. "The television crews were doing live spots at eleven. And I was thinking."

"Why couldn't it have waited until the morning, then?"

"The press is still dogging me. They would have been around. Right now they're making last call."

Bryant's badge gained us entry through a police guard. We crossed the yellow DO NOT CROSS police tape that surrounded Vincent's Victorian house, and went inside. Bryant rubbed his hands and yawned while I walked around. It was full of Vincent's oddments, but the place wasn't as messy as his loft.

I walked through the kitchen, and living room, and family room. Bryant tagged along, a sleepy shadow, groaning just a little as we walked upstairs. I got a little angry at human nature. I had shot someone fourteen hours earlier, had lived a day of coffee, recriminations, more coffee, too much smoke, and hoarseness. I wanted that warm shoulder, and an end to the day and all the business of it, but there were a few things I had to see. Or not see.

There were three bedrooms. I walked through the first two, pushed a few papers, and opened a few closets. Then

I went into the master bedroom. Bryant bumped into me as I left. I had only needed the one glance.

"Aren't you going to look any more?" he asked.

"No."

"Are we leaving?"

"Yes."

Our drive back was also quiet. Bryant tried to sleep. I broke our silence at his house and asked him for one more favor. He told me he'd see what he could see. And then also told me I looked like hell, and should get some sleep.

I decided to go back to my own place. I slept for a few hours, and I didn't have my dream, but I still looked like hell when I got up in the morning. Miss Tuntland was handling all my calls, and I was sorry for all the bother I was putting her through. I thought of calling her, but decided to hold off for a few hours. There was someone I still had to see.

I didn't ring the bell. Her door was unlocked. Maybe she was expecting some deliveries.

Of course, she didn't hear me. She was bent over at work on one of her quilts. I watched her work for a few minutes, and then she finally noticed me.

"Stuart!" she cried, and then ran and hugged me.

Habit closed my arms around her for a second. Revulsion dropped them to my sides.

Ellen searched my eyes. "I read the paper," she said. "It must have been so horrible."

I felt my arm move on its own accord, felt it point at her and twist into the appropriate word. She knew the sign, and stepped away from me. The sign had been my companion on and off since I had awakened that morning. It had a mind of its own, a mind I couldn't control yet. But with the announcement made, I proceeded.

"How did you get the scar on your left ear?" I asked.

She turned away from me, tried to collect her thoughts. I grabbed her shoulders and made her face my lips.

"Tell me," I said.

"It happened years ago," she said.

"How?"

"An accident. I fell . . ."

"You're a liar."

"Stuart, I don't understand."

"I visited Vincent's house yesterday. Hanging in his bedroom is a quilt. Your quilt."

"I've sold my quilts all over . . ."

"I made a few calls. The two of you were lovers. It happened quickly, almost casually, but Vincent was definitely attracted to you."

I took my hand from her right shoulder and grabbed her left ear. "It was almost a fatal attraction, wasn't it?"

"Stuart, I . . ."

"You had a voice to talk your way through Vincent's fantasies. You saved your ears, and maybe your life, but you knew how dangerous he was. And you still hated Anita."

She was trying to close her eyes, trying to turn her head from me, but I wouldn't let her.

"Vincent said an artist friend recommended Anita. You were that artist friend. But how much of a Judas goat were you? Did you pretend a reconciliation with her?"

She was sobbing now. Her body was shaking in my hands, begging to be held and comforted.

"I didn't mean for her to die," Ellen said. "It was just that she was so high and mighty. I thought Vincent might scare her . . ."

"Just maybe scar or disfigure her," I said.

"It wasn't like that."

"You knew who killed her. You knew what happened. And you never said anything."

"I didn't want to look guilty."

"You even left that newspaper for me in my office. Why?"

"I could tell you were obsessed with Anita. One of my classmates mentioned seeing her in that paper. I wanted to show you what kind of woman she was. I wanted you to see, and forget her."

"I doubt whether the DA will try to prosecute you," I said. "But I'm going to tell him about your involvement and silence. He'll probably call it circumstantial and forget about it."

"And what will you call it?" she asked.

I was going to speak, but my arm acted on its own again, and made the sign that would always stand between us. I turned away and started walking toward my car.

She called to me between her sobs. She said, "Stuart, I love you."

But it was my turn to be deaf.

The Scotch was in my left hand. It was safer there. The phone was cradled next to my ear, and I was looking over a fireplace that didn't have a fire. Reporters were still staking out the front of the house, which would give me an excuse not to go out for a few days. A harried Miss Tuntland answered my call on the twentieth ring. There was no friendliness in her "Hello," and that was a first.

"I'm sorry to be making your life a hell," I said.

"It's not your fault."

Her voice was soft. Women forgive so much more graciously and easily than men.

"So how can I make this up to you?"

"Ask me in a few days. There are lots of calls coming in now and I'm sure they're all for you. Do you want to hold?"

"No. Let's just talk for a minute."

"Are you all right?"

"Was I ever?"

"You know what I mean."

"I feel better talking with you."

"Thank you, but you're still evading the question."

"You sound like Norman."

"He's one of your million messages. He wants to see you."

"I can't see anyone for a few days, Miss Tuntland. You'll have to tell them that. I'm trying to get over something."

"I understand."

She didn't, but she couldn't see, didn't know the urge to sign was coming on me even as we spoke. I took a gulp of the Glenfiddich and clenched my right hand.

"How's your painting coming along, Miss Tuntland?"

She sounded surprised, and didn't know how to answer. "Fine."

"What do you paint?"

"Bucolic scenes mostly. Rustic gardens and meadows. Places far from the madness."

"I'd like to buy one of your paintings."

"You'd be my first sale."

"I know good art when I hear it."

"I'll bet you don't have a painting in your house."

"Wrong. I'm looking at one right now. It was delivered today by my friend Don Bryant."

"Is he an artist?"

"No. A cop."

"What kind of painting is it?"

I looked at the canvas. It didn't have a frame yet, and probably never would. Vincent's blood already looked faded, and it wasn't even thirty hours old.

"It's modern, I guess."

I felt the urge again. My left hand grabbed my right arm, grabbed it and tried to stop it. It wasn't entirely successful, and I dropped the phone in my struggle. When my fit was over, I picked it up.

"I'm sorry, Miss Tuntland. I was clumsy. And I should let you get back to your work."

She didn't want to break our connection, tried to keep me talking.

"What's your painting titled, Mr. Winter?"

But the word didn't come from my lips. It rose from my hand. My right index finger jabbed out and then pushed forward under my left palm, and this time I didn't try to stop it.

ELLIOTT ROOSEVELT'S
DELIGHTFUL MYSTERY SERIES

MURDER IN THE ROSE GARDEN
70529-X/$4.95US/$5.95Can

MURDER IN THE OVAL OFFICE
70528-1/$4.99US/$5.99Can

MURDER AND THE FIRST LADY
69937-0/$4.99US/$5.99Can

THE HYDE PARK MURDER
70058-1/$4.50US/$5.50Can

MURDER AT HOBCAW BARONY
70021-2/$4.50US/$5.50Can

THE WHITE HOUSE PANTRY MURDER
70404-8/$4.50US/$5.50Can

MURDER AT THE PALACE
70405-6/$4.99US/$5.99Can

MURDER IN THE BLUE ROOM
71237-7/$4.99US/$5.99Can

FOLLOW IN THE FOOTSTEPS OF
DETECTIVE J.P. BEAUMONT
WITH FAST-PACED MYSTERIES
BY J.A. JANCE

UNTIL PROVEN GUILTY   89638-9/$4.50 US/$5.50 CAN

INJUSTICE FOR ALL   89641-9/$4.50 US/$5.50 CAN

TRIAL BY FURY   75138-0/$3.95 US/$4.95 CAN

TAKING THE FIFTH   75139-9/$4.50 US/$5.50 CAN

IMPROBABLE CAUSE   75412-6/$4.50 US/$5.50 CAN

A MORE PERFECT UNION 75413-4/$4.50 US/$5.50 CAN

DISMISSED WITH PREJUDICE
                          75547-5/$4.99 US/$5.99 CAN

MINOR IN POSSESSION   75546-7/$4.50 US/$5.50 CAN

PAYMENT IN KIND   75836-9/$4.50 US/$5.50 CAN

Coming Soon
WITHOUT DUE PROCESS

And also by J.A. Jance
HOUR OF THE HUNTER   71107-9/$4.99 US/$5.99 CAN